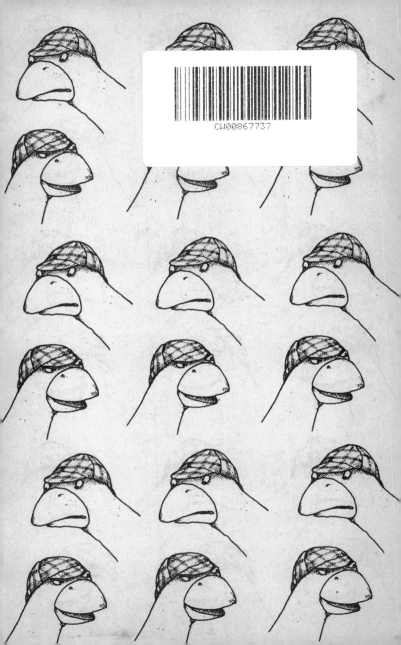

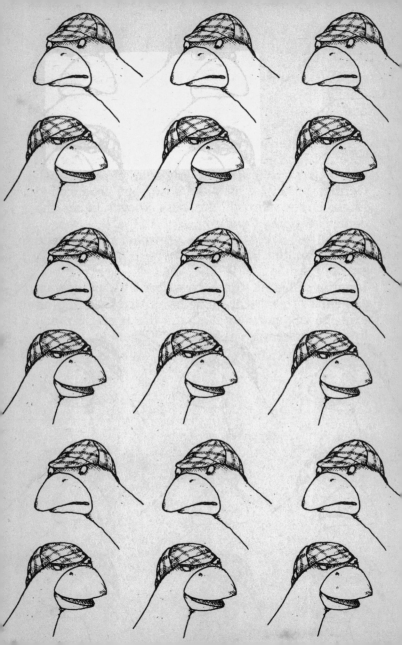

David Henry Wilson was born in London and educated at Dulwich College and Pembroke College, Cambridge. He lectures at the universities of Bristol and Konstanz, Germany where he founded the student theatre.

His children's books have been translated into several languages, and his novel *The Coachman Rat* has been acclaimed in England, America and Germany. Many of his plays have been produced in England and abroad, the best known being the comedy *Gas and Candles*.

He is married, with three grown-up children and lives in Taunton, Somerset.

Jonathan Allen is himself a writer with an original and bizarre sense of humour, as well as being an exceptionally talented illustrator. He is married and lives in London with a cat called William.

In memory of Bess and Bill

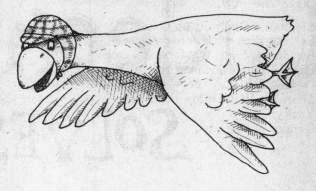

Gideon ·
SOLVES
Greatest

Piper Original published by
Pan Macmillan

Gander

THE WORLD'S

Mysteries

by DAVID HENRY WILSON

drawings by Jonathan Allen

Children's Books

First published 1993 by
PAN MACMILLAN CHILDREN'S BOOKS
a division of Pan Macmillan Publishers Limited
Cavaye Place London SW10 9PG
and Basingstoke
Associated companies throughout the world

9 8 7 6 5 4 3 2

A CIP catalogue record for this book, is available from
the British Library

ISBN 0 330 325507

Printed and bound in Great Britain by
Cox & Wyman Ltd, Reading, Berkshire

Gideon Gander solves
THE WORLD'S GREATEST MYSTERIES

"Gideon Gander is the greatest detective in the world."   *Gideon Gander last year*

"Gideon Gander is still the greatest detective in the world."   *Gideon Gander this year*

My name is Gideon Gander, and I need no introduction from me. My first book, modestly called *Gander of the Yard,* has been a huge success and has made me famous. I have had fan mail from all over the world – the letter wasn't very clearly addressed and took a year to get here.

This is my new book, with some more of my amazing cases. I shall reveal who ate Miss Muffet's curds and whey, who stole Lucy Lurse's purse, the real identity of Georgie Porgie, and what the black sheep really did with his three bags of wool. You'll meet His Majesty the King, and the Queen's father, Old King Cole, and will learn all about Solomon Grundy's strange marriage.

It's lucky for Mother Goose that she's married to me and not to Solomon Grundy. I'm a wonderful husband and father, and as well as allowing her to look after all the goslings, I let her give as many lessons as possible to Gary, our youngest, who would be a walking disaster, if he knew how to walk.

We live in Farmer Green's yard. Farmer Green has a shotgun, a strange way of talking, and a wife named Mrs Green. Mrs Green has a lot of nice things in the kitchen, a not-so-nice broom-handle, and two children. Their names are Johnny and Bo-Peep.

Wolfie commits nearly all the crimes in our village, but he says he doesn't. Spiffy the Sparrow doesn't commit nearly all the crimes in our village, but he says he does. This makes my job very difficult, but I solve every case, including the unsolved mystery of where, oh where, the little dog went.

I hope you'll enjoy these stories, and will tell everybody else about them so that everybody else can enjoy them, too. They are certainly the best stories ever written, and so as well as being the greatest detective in the world, I must be the greatest story-teller in the world, too. I ought to write that down.

"Gideon Gander is the greatest story-teller in the world."

                                        Gideon Gander

List of Cases

Who Killed Solomon Grundy?

My investigation into the death of Solomon
Grundy began when he died. Even I can't investigate someone's death until they're dead, and
indeed if Solomon Grundy hadn't died, I would
never have investigated his death at all. That
would have been a pity (for me – maybe not for
Solomon Grundy) as it is one of my most famous
cases.

It all began on a Saturday. Gary Gosling, our youngest, was having a honking lesson. Gary has to have lessons in everything. When he was born, we even had to teach him how to break open his egg, though if we'd known then what we know now, we probably wouldn't have bothered. I hate giving Gary lessons, and so I suddenly stopped in mid honk.

"What was that?" I asked.

"Half a honk," said Mother Goose.

"No, no," I said. "I heard a noise in the house. I think I'd better go and investigate."

And before Mother Goose could say "Come back!" I'd gone forth. I hadn't actually heard a noise, but I'll do anything to get away from Gary.

As it happened, there *was* a noise in the house. Mrs Green was crying, and Farmer Green was saying:

"Don't cry, dry your eye, everybody has to die."

"Poor Solomon," sobbed Mrs Green. "What could have killed him?"

"I'll bet my life it's all that strife with his wife," said Farmer Green.

If Mrs Green didn't know what had killed Solomon, who better to find out than the great detective himself? I marched into the living room.

"I'll take the case," I said. "Who was Solomon?"

"He was my brother," sobbed Mrs Green.

"Ah!" I said. "Solomon Green."

"No," said Mrs Green. "Solomon Grundy."

"One moment," I said. "If he's your brother, he should have the same name as you."

I had already discovered the first mistake.

"Haven't you heard, you absurd bird," said Farmer Green, "that a man and his dame take the same name?"

The first mistake had actually been mine, but there was no need for Farmer Green to be so rude. I am not an absurd bird.

"He was such a kind and gentle person," said Mrs Green. "He didn't deserve such a cruel fate."

Although she didn't realize it, she had given me the first clue. Who in this world was cruel enough to kill kind, gentle Solomon Grundy? One name came to mind immediately: Wolfie. He'd kill anyone and anything if he thought it would make someone unhappy.

3

I left the Greens and returned to Mother Goose. She was still with little Gary, who was saying "knoh, knoh, knoh".

"Not quite, dear," said Mother Goose. "It's 'honk', not 'knoh'."

"Maybe he should turn round and face the other way," I said.

It was another good piece of thinking. Unfortunately, when Gary tried to turn round, he fell over. He was going to need a lesson in turning round, and I certainly didn't have time for that. I quickly told Mother Goose about the new case and about my theory.

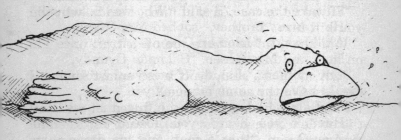

"But why do you suspect Wolfie?" she asked.

"I always suspect Wolfie," I replied.

It was true.

Wolfie was his usual nasty self.

"Well, well," he said, "if it isn't my old friend Giddy Goose."

"Gideon Gander," I said. He always gets my name wrong.

"Still pretending to be a detective, are you?" he sneered.

"I *am* a detective," I said.

"OK," he said, "then solve a mystery for me."

"What mystery?" I asked.

"The mystery," he said, "of how a silly goose comes to call himself a great detective."

Then he howled with laughter as if he'd just made a joke.

"All right, you evil monster," I said. (I can be pretty rude myself when I'm angry.) "Now just tell me why you murdered Solomon Grundy?"

That stopped him laughing.

"Solomon who?" he asked.

"Solomon Grundy," I replied.

"Grundy, Grundy," said Wolfie, pretending he'd never heard of him. "I've never heard of him."

"If you've never heard of him," I said, "why did you kill him?"

It takes a lot to shake me off a trail once I'm on it.

"OK, OK," he said, "you're too smart for me. I confess. Come and arrest me."

I believed his confession. It fitted in with all the evidence I had so far. But I wasn't so keen on arresting him, since I could well be the one to finish up inside.

5

"No thanks, Wolfie," I said. "I'll get Farmer Green to arrest you."

"In that case," said Wolfie, "I didn't do it."

"But you just confessed that you did," I said. I enjoy a good battle of wits, and it's always a pleasure to outsmart Wolfie.

"Prove it," he said. "Where are your witnesses?"

He was right. By sheer luck, it looked as though this time Wolfie had outsmarted me.

"I'm a witness!"

It was a moment of unexpected triumph. Out of the trees came my old friend Spiffy the Sparrow.

"I 'eard 'im," said Spiffy, "I 'eard 'im confess."

And so I had outsmarted Wolfie yet again.

"Got you this time, Wolfie," I said.

"An' I'll tell yer somefink else," said Spiffy.

"What's that, Spiffy?" I asked.

"'E's lyin'," said Spiffy.

I was not surprised. Wolfie has always been a liar. Lying is as natural to Wolfie as murder and being rude.

"That's typical!" I said. "A murderer *and* a liar, eh, Wolfie?"

"No," said Wolfie. "Just a liar."

He was still trying to outsmart me, and I felt almost sorry for him.

"Bad luck, Wolfie," I said, "but Spiffy's my witness. You're a murderer *and* a liar."

"I was lying," said Wolfie, "when I said I'd killed Solomon Grundy. I didn't kill him. That makes me a liar and an un-murderer."

I found this a little hard to follow.

"Is all this true, Spiffy?" I asked.

"Is all wot true?" asked Spiffy.

"What Wolfie said," I replied.

"I didn't unnerstan' wot 'e said," replied Spiffy.

Nor did I. I'd been hoping that Spiffy had.

"Let's get this straight, Wolfie," I said. "Are you telling me you're not the murderer?"

"I am," said Wolfie, "and I'm not."

"What do you mean?" I asked.

"I am telling you," said Wolfie, "and I'm not the murderer."

"Course 'e ain't the murderer," said Spiffy. "I am."

This was a real surprise. My star witness had suddenly turned out to be the criminal.

"You killed Solomon Grundy?" I cried.

"Killed 'im dead as a breadcrumb," said Spiffy.

"How did you kill him, Spiffy?" asked Wolfie, grinning for some reason.

It was a good question, and I wished I'd asked it myself.

"Ah well," said Spiffy, "'e ... um ... stopped breavin', didn'e?"

"And how did you stop him?" asked Wolfie.

7

"I'll ask the questions if you don't mind!" I snapped. I'd had enough of Wolfie's interference. "Now then, Spiffy, think carefully. How did you stop Solomon Grundy from breathing?"

To be honest, I didn't think it mattered very much how Spiffy had stopped Solomon from breathing. The fact is that anyone who stops breathing will soon be dead.

"I picked 'im up," said Spiffy, "an 'eld 'im upside down till all the air 'ad fallen out of 'is nose."

Wolfie let out a loud laugh.

"I don't see anything funny in this, Wolfie," I said sharply. "Mrs Green's brother is dead, and that's no laughing matter."

Wolfie laughed even louder, turned over on his back, and waved his legs in the air.

"Do you know what he's laughing at, Spiffy?" I asked.

" 'Aven't a clue," said Spiffy.

Wolfie, when he'd finally managed to roll on to his front again, asked Spiffy how a tiny sparrow could lift a full-grown man into the air and hold him upside down. Spiffy nodded in my direction:

"Let Giddy ask the questions," he said. " 'E's the detective."

He was right, and I was glad he'd put Wolfie in his place. All the same, Wolfie's question raised a few questions, and so I asked them.

"Spiffy," I said, "how could a tiny sparrow lift a full-grown man into the air and hold him upside down?"

There was a long silence, and then finally Spiffy came up with the answer: "Wiv difficulty," he said.

It was at this moment that I remembered something: Spiffy had lied to me before. He had, for instance, confessed to killing Cock Robin, to stealing Bo-Peep's sheep, and to taking Doggy's bone from Mother Hubbard's cupboard. But he hadn't committed any of those crimes. And now he'd been lying again.

This was a bitter disappointment. If Wolfie hadn't killed Solomon Grundy, and Spiffy hadn't killed Solomon Grundy, then who had? Twice I'd come close to solving the mystery, and twice I'd had the solution taken away by witnesses lying. Or telling the truth. It was all very confusing.

I needed some more information. Such as, who killed Solomon Grundy. I decided that I would question Mrs Green in the morning.

That night I didn't get a wink of sleep. Gary kept knohing in his dreams, and when I woke him up in order to stop him, he couldn't get his eyes closed again. If his right eye was shut, his left eye was open, and if his left eye was open, he couldn't close his beak. I'd have done better to leave him knohing.

Although I hadn't slept all night, I was surprised to be woken up by a lot of cars arriving at the Greens' house. Mother Goose and the goslings were already in the yard having breakfast – or in Gary's case, aiming to have breakfast, and missing.

I noticed that the people going into the house were all wearing black.

"Interesting," I said. "These people are all wearing black. I suspect that someone has died."

"Of course someone's died," said Mother Goose.

"Who?" I asked.

"Solomon Grundy," she said.

She was right. I'd forgotten about him. It was lucky that she reminded me, because just as she was asking me to give Gary a swallowing lesson, I remembered my plan to question Mrs Green. At once I hurried off to the house.

Mrs Green was in the kitchen, together with Bo-Peep and another lady whom I didn't know. They were all busy making sandwiches and cakes.

"Good morning, Mrs Green," I said. "I'm afraid I must interrupt you for a moment."

"What is it, Gideon?" she asked.

"Just a few vital questions," I replied.

"What sort of questions?" she asked.

"First of all," I said, "who killed Solomon Grundy?"

She looked at me with astonishment all over her face. I knew at once that she could not answer my question, and so I immediately asked her another. I had suddenly remembered something Farmer Green had said to her the previous day.

"May I remind you, Mrs Green," I said, "of your husband's remark yesterday? His words were: 'I'll bet my life it's all that strife with his wife'."

Then something very strange happened. For no reason, the lady whom I did not know uttered a piercing scream and rushed out of the kitchen.

"What's the matter with her?" I asked.

"You stupid goose!" cried Mrs Green, and rushed out after the lady.

I was quite shocked by this. As Mrs Green well knows, I am neither stupid nor a goose.

"Oh dear, Giddy," said Bo-Peep, "you've done it now. That was Mrs Grundy."

"Who's Mrs Grundy?" I asked.

"Solomon Grundy's wife," she said.

This was unexpected. But Bo-Peep's simple statement immediately brought two things into my mind. Firstly, she'd made a mistake.

"Don't you mean Solomon Grundy's widow?" I said.

11

Such details can change the course of a case.

Secondly, Bo-Peep's words gave me the clue that I had been looking for. An ordinary detective would never have spotted it, but Gideon Gander is no ordinary detective. Let me repeat the facts. Farmer Green had said, "I'll bet my life it's all that strife with his wife." When I reminded Mrs Green of these words, Mrs Grundy uttered a piercing scream and rushed out of the kitchen. Link these facts together, and you will learn the identity of Solomon Grundy's murderer.

I will explain it to you. Ask yourself *why* Mrs Grundy screamed and left the kitchen. It could only be because she knew I was on to her. What could be more natural than a murderer, hearing herself accused, uttering a piercing scream and rushing away? In her position, I would have done the same.

Why had she killed him? When you think of Mother Goose, it's hard to imagine any wife wanting to kill her husband. But not all wives have husbands like Gideon Gander.

Knowing the name of the murderer is one thing, and proving it is another, as I have often found with Wolfie. And Spiffy. It would help me if I knew how Mr Grundy had died, but I was still too upset by the "stupid goose" business to ask the Greens or Mrs Grundy. I did ask Bo-Peep, but she didn't know.

"Perhaps," I said, "I could see the body."

"That would be difficult," she said.

"Why?" I asked.

"We buried it this morning," said Bo-Peep.

It was another clue. You don't bury something unless you've got something to hide. What was

Mrs Grundy hiding? There was only one way to find out. I went to the churchyard. This served two vital purposes: to search for clues, and not to be near Gary at lunchtime.

Bo-Peep had been right – I couldn't see the body. But what I did see was even more useful, for it told me several important facts. I don't think the body would have told me any facts at all. It was Mr Grundy's gravestone that I saw, and written on it were the following words:

Solomon Grundy,
Born on a Monday,
Christened on Tuesday,
Married on Wednesday,
Took ill on Thursday,
Worse on Friday,
Died on Saturday,
Buried on Sunday.
This is the end
Of Solomon Grundy.

The first thing I noticed was how young Mr Grundy was when he got married. I worked it out that he was just two days old, which is far too early for anyone to settle down. How can a two-day-old look after a wife? I'm a mature and extremely intelligent adult, but even I sometimes have difficulty coping with my wife, not to mention my family, and especially not to mention young Gary. Little Mr Grundy might even have been another Gary, in which case it was hardly surprising that Mrs Grundy had murdered him.

It certainly wasn't surprising that the marriage had been full of strife. Mr and Mrs Grundy would

not have been able to speak properly to each other, since two-day-old human beings can't even talk. All Mr Grundy could have done was drink milk. Mrs Grundy must have taken her husband on her lap, fed him from the bottle, changed his nappies, and said gaga, baba, mama to him a hundred times. *He* might have enjoyed it. There's a lot to be said for having someone look after you day and night, and I wouldn't mind being a bit more looked after myself. But husbands have to protect their families. What protection could a tiny pink Grundy have given to Mrs Grundy? Or to their children? Would you feel safe if your father was just two days old?

There was another important clue on the gravestone: the Grundys had been married on Wednesday, and Mr Grundy had become ill the very next day. He was worse the day after, and dead the day after that, which was yesterday. It was my belief that Mr Grundy's illness had caused his death, and his illness had begun the day after his wedding. What, then, had Mrs Grundy put in her husband's feeding bottle?

When I got home, I told my wife what I had discovered.

"What makes you think," she asked, "that it was all in the same week?"

"That what was all in the same week?" I asked.

"He was probably born on a Monday, christened a few weeks later on a Tuesday, and married twenty-five years later on a Wednesday," said Mother Goose.

Now this hadn't occurred to me, and I wasn't too pleased that it had occurred to Mother Goose. If she was right, it would change my whole theory about the Grundys' marriage, and indeed about Mr Grundy's death. It was clear that I would have to talk to Mrs Grundy herself. I needed to know how old Mr Grundy was when they got married, how he had died, and why she had killed him. If I could find the answers to those three questions, the mystery would be solved.

My chance came a few days later. I had taken to visiting Mr Grundy's grave every day, round about Gary's lesson time. I entered the churchyard, and saw Mrs Grundy kneeling beside her husband's grave. I noticed that she was crying – another sign of guilt.

"Good morning, Mrs Grundy," I said.

It was a clever way to open the conversation. I like to put my suspects at ease before I pounce on them.

"It's a pleasant surprise to meet you here," I said.

The expression on her face was one of recognition and fear. She must have remembered the way I exposed her guilt in the kitchen. I needed to calm her.

"Do you come here often?" I asked.

"Please leave me alone," she said.

It was yet another proof of her guilt. Why else would she want to get rid of me?

"I will in a moment, Mrs Grundy," I said. "But first I must ask you one or two questions."

She looked – as I thought, rather despairingly – from the grave to me and then back at the grave. She could see there was no escape.

"Will you go away if I answer?" she asked.

"Of course," I said.

"What do you want to know, then?"

"First of all, Mrs Grundy, how old was Mr Grundy when you married him?"

"Twenty-five," she replied.

This fitted in well with what Mother Goose and I had calculated.

"Good," I said. "In that case, you didn't have to change his nappies."

She looked puzzled, but ordinary people often are puzzled at how we detectives work things out.

"Now secondly, Mrs Grundy, I'd like to know how Mr Grundy died."

"He had a heart attack," she said.

This was not quite the answer I had expected. A heart attack is not usually a murder weapon.

"Are you sure?" I asked.

"Of course I'm sure," she said. "He had an attack on Thursday, and another on Friday, and he died on Saturday."

She began to cry again.

"In the same week?" I asked.

"Yes," she replied. "It all happened last week."

So I'd been right after all. It *was* the same week. And yet she'd said Mr Grundy had been twenty-five when he'd married her. Already her story was falling apart. But I still had my third question to ask, and it was one that had to be put with the utmost tact. I gazed into her tear-stained face.

"Mrs Grundy," I said, "why did you kill him?"

Again her response was unexpected.

"Oh please go away!" she cried. "Can't you see how unhappy I am?"

I could. A bad conscience is a terrible thing. On the other hand, if Mr Grundy had died from a heart attack, why should she have a bad conscience? I decided to talk the whole thing over with my wife. It often helps to discuss such cases with someone, and Mother Goose is a good listener. I told her everything that had happened in the churchyard.

"It doesn't make sense," I concluded. "She says it was the same week, yet he was twenty-five when he married her. And how could he have died of a heart attack if she murdered him? A heart attack is not a murder weapon."

"Then maybe," she said, "Mr Grundy wasn't murdered. If he'd been murdered, the police would have investigated the case. As for the heart attacks, they may have been in the same week but the rest happened at different times."

I had been absolutely right. Talking things over does help. Until now none of us had thought of the possibility that Mr Grundy had been born on a Monday, christened some weeks later on a Tueday, married Mrs Grundy twenty-five years later on a Wednesday, and then some years after that had his heart attacks and his death. And the conversation with Mother Goose had put another amazing thought into my head.

Solomon Grundy had not been murdered. His death, which an ordinary detective would have thought was caused by murder, had in fact been brought about by a heart attack, and, despite Farmer Green's understandable suspicion that Mrs Grundy had killed her husband, I had finally proved that she was innocent.

I put this idea to Mother Goose.

"Well done, dear," she said. "You have a gift for making the obvious seem like a great discovery."

It's nice to be appreciated.

"It seems to me," I said to Mother Goose, "that I can close the file on this case. But I must let Mrs Green know my findings."

Mrs Green was in the kitchen.

"Hello, Mrs Green," I said.

"Hello, Gideon," she replied.

I was pleased at her response. The last time we'd spoken, she'd been rather rude to me, and the memory was still a little painful.

"I thought you'd like to know," I said, "that I've solved the Grundy mystery."

"Oh, and what's that?" she asked.

"You'll be relieved to hear," I continued, "that Mrs Grundy didn't murder your brother after all."

She looked surprised. No doubt the idea had got fixed in her mind, and so she found it difficult to accept the truth.

"Whatever gave you that idea?" she asked.

"Quite simply," I said, "he died of a heart attack."

It was a great moment, and I was tempted to add, "So who's a stupid goose now?" But I didn't. One doesn't say that kind of thing to Mrs Green. Instead, I left the kitchen feeling well pleased with myself.

You may wonder why this case has gone down in history as something so special, since there was no crime and there was no criminal. But that is precisely what makes it so special. By revealing that Mr Grundy had not been murdered, I was able to provide a happy ending for everyone concerned. The Greens, Wolfie (unfortunately), Spiffy, and Mrs Grundy herself all had cause to be grateful to me. And I expect Mr Grundy would have been grateful, too, if he'd lived to tell the tale.

Georgie Porgie

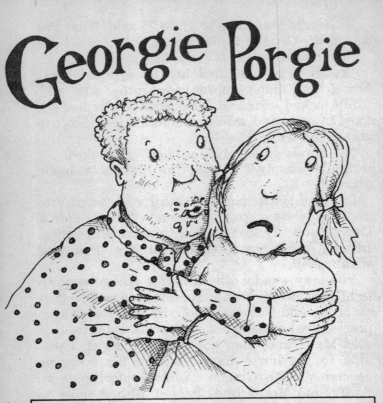

Little Bo-Peep and her brother Johnny Green both went to the village school, and it was there that a very strange crime took place. I heard about it when Bo-Peep came home crying, with the news that someone called Georgie Porgie had gone round kissing all the girls.

"He was horrible!" sobbed Bo-Peep. "He was carrying a pudding and a pie, and he kept kissing us and leaving great big mouthfuls of pudding or pie on our faces! Yuck!"

"Calm down, dear," said Mrs Green, "and tell me what happened."

"It was break-time for us girls," said Bo-Peep, "and we were playing in the playground when Georgie Porgie came and started kissing us."

"Who is this Georgie Porgie?" asked Mrs Green.

"We don't know," said Bo-Peep. "We'd never seen him before, but he kissed Miss Muffet, and Lucy Lurse, and Kitty Fisher, and Contrary Mary, and then he kissed me!"

"Didn't you call the teacher?" asked Mrs Green.

"No," said Bo-Peep. "Because just then the boys came out to play, and Georgie Porgie ran away."

"Did you see him, Johnny?" asked Mrs Green.

"No," said Johnny. "He must have run away when he saw us boys coming. We're tough, we boys are. We wouldn't have let him kiss *us*."

It was clearly a case for Gander of the Yard.

"Don't worry, Mrs Green," I said. "Leave it to me. I'll get straight on the trail."

Off I went.

"Hadn't you better find out what he looks like?" called Mrs Green.

21

Back I came. She was right, it might be useful.

"He's fat and horrible," said Bo-Peep. "He's got a fat tummy and horrible breath, and he's got all this pudding and pie, and he's got freckles and red cheeks and red hair and a big bottom. And he's wearing short yellow trousers and a spotty pink shirt."

It wasn't a lot to go on. But there were a few details in her story that reminded me of one possible suspect. Who would be nasty enough to kiss the girls, and coward enough to run away when the boys came out to play? I had to admit that Wolfie wasn't fat, freckled, red-cheeked, red-haired or big-bottomed, and he didn't normally wear yellow shorts or spotty pink shirts, but he was certainly horrible and had horrible breath. The rest could have been a clever disguise.

When I got to Wolfie's, the case took its first surprising turn. Wolfie usually denies everything, but this time, when I accused him of kissing all the girls, to my amazement he immediately confessed.

"Sure," he said, "I'm always kissing the girls. And the girls are always kissing me. I'm irresistible. I can't help it. I have this natural charm."

"Natural charm?" I said. "All the girls were crying. Some charm!"

"Crying?" said Wolfie. "No, they only cry when I leave them. 'More!' they cry. 'Give us more, Wolfie! Don't leave us!' "

"And you left mouthfuls of pudding and pie all over their faces," I said. "Is that part of your charm as well?"

"Pudding and pie?" echoed Wolfie. "Never touch 'em."

"And you ran away when the boys came out to play."

"Hold on, hold on," said Wolfie. "When I'm around, it's the boys that run away. Just who are we talking about here?"

"We're talking," I said, "about Georgie Porgie."

"And who's Georgie Porgie?"

"Georgie Porgie," I said, "is the name you used when you went to the school and kissed the girls and made them cry."

"Listen, Goosey," said Wolfie, "if I wanted to use another name, do you think I'd use a flabby, podgy, blubbery name like Georgie Porgie?"

"Well if it wasn't you, Wolfie, who was it?"

"Hey, hey, Goosey, I'm not the detective, right?"

He *was* right. I was the detective. But Wolfie

was the only suspect I had, and if he wasn't Georgie Porgie, then I had a difficult case on my hands.

"If he was walking around with pudding and pie," said Wolfie, "why don't you ask the pieman?"

It was a good idea, but I didn't want to let Wolfie know that it was a good idea, otherwise he'd be boasting for weeks that he'd had a good idea.

"That's a silly idea, Wolfie," I said. "The pieman is called the pieman, not Georgie Porgie."

"But he may know your Georgie Porgie," said Wolfie.

"On the other hand," I snapped, "he may not."

This time I was right. Wolfie knew he was beaten. He shrugged his shoulders, yawned, and invited me in for tea. What he had in mind was *his* tea.

Instead, I went to the pieman's shop. I knew the pieman couldn't be Georgie Porgie, because he had a thin bottom, but I'd worked it out that George Porgie must have got his pudding and pie from someone. That someone could be the pieman.

"Hello, Mr Gideon," said the pieman. "Have you come for some hot cross buns?"

24

"Not today, pieman," I said. "I'm looking for Georgie Porgie."

But the pieman had never heard of Georgie Porgie.

"He must have got his pudding and pie from someone," I said. "Puddings and pies don't grow on trees, pieman, they have to be made."

"I know that, Mr Gideon," said the pieman. "I'm the man who makes them."

"Then who made Georgie Porgie's pudding and pie?" I asked.

"I don't know," he said.

He was not being very helpful. If anyone should know who makes somebody's puddings and pies, it ought to be the pieman. I suspected that he was hiding something.

"Not at all, Mr Gideon," he said. "All my puddings and pies are on display."

"You're holding something back," I persisted.

"No, Mr Gideon," he said. "It's true one or two of my pies might not contain quite what they're supposed to contain, but I'm not holding any of them back."

He seemed an honest enough man. But I wasn't looking for an honest man. I was looking for a criminal.

"Who else makes puddings and pies, apart from you?" I asked.

"Some of the mothers do," said the pieman. "Mrs Horner round the corner makes Christmas pies that are almost as good as mine."

"Mrs Horner, eh?" I said. "Does she have a son?"

"Why yes, she does," said the pieman. "Little Jack."

It was a clue at last. Jack began with the same

sound as Georgie, and if Jack Horner was a pie-eater, my search could be over. I knocked on the Horners' door, and it was opened by a very big man with a bristling moustache and bushy eyebrows.

"What do you want?" he growled.

"Good afternoon," I said. "Do I have the pleasure of addressing Little Jack Horner?"

"No," he said.

This was unexpected. I checked the number on the door, and it was certainly the address the pieman had given me.

"Are you sure?" I asked.

"Who are you?" he asked.

He hadn't answered my question. That is often a sign of guilt. This man's attitude was very suspicious. He was not fat or freckled or red-cheeked or red-haired, and he wasn't wearing yellow shorts or a spotty pink shirt. But he was certainly horrible, and he had a very big bottom.

"Well?" he growled. "Who are you and what do you want?"

"My name is Gideon Gander," I replied.

I waited for him to react. Most people when they hear my name say, "Oh, the famous detective!" or "I'm honoured to meet you, sir," or "I confess! I did it!" But this man didn't react at all. He just stood there and scowled.

"Well?" he growled again.

"I'm the famous detective," I said.

"Never heard of you," he said.

He was obviously a criminal. I have an instinct for these things.

"I was told," I said icily, "that Little Jack Horner lived here."

"So he does," said the man. "What do you want with him?"

Just then a tiny woman poked her head into the hall.

"Who is it, Henry?" she asked.

"Some goose asking about Little Jack," replied the man.

"I'm not a goose," I said. "I'm a gander."

The tiny woman came to the door and stood next to the huge man. I needed two necks to look at them.

"Little Jack's eating his Christmas pie," she said.

It was a bad mistake.

"That's impossible," I said. "It isn't Christmas."

"Little Jack has Christmas pie every day," she said. "He loves his mother's Christmas pie."

She had let slip an important fact. She was Little Jack's mother. It was therefore possible that the big man was Little Jack's father. This might explain why he had denied being Little Jack himself.

But there was another, even more important fact: Little Jack ate Christmas pie every day. Christmas pie is a rich pie, and rich pies are fattening, and it wouldn't surprise me if Christmas pies didn't give people freckles and red hair and big bottoms. I had to see Little Jack.

"What do you want to see him for?" asked the tiny lady.

"I'm investigating a case," I said, "and he may be able to help me with my enquiries."

"Are you a detective, then?" she asked.

"I'm none other than Gideon Gander," I replied.

"How do you do?" she said. "And are you a detective?"

At this moment a tiny boy came running into the hall. He was even tinier than tiny. He was teeny. He was as teeny compared to the woman as the woman was tiny compared to the man.

"Mummy, Mummy!" he cried. "Daddy, Daddy! I've finished my pie, I've finished it, I've finished it! And do you know what I found in it, Mummy and Daddy, do you know what I found? I found a plum! I did, I did! A plum! I pulled it out with my thumb! I put in my thumb, and I pulled out the plum! Oh, aren't I a good boy, Mummy and Daddy? Mummy and Daddy, aren't I good? Oh, I am a good boy! What a good boy I am! And I can't wait till tomorrow for another Christmas pie, Mummy, because I love your Christmas pies, and maybe tomorrow, Mummy and Daddy, I'll find another plum and pull it out with my thumb and who's this?"

"This is a goose, dear," said the tiny woman.

"Are you going to make a pie with him, Mummy?" asked the teeny boy.

I didn't like this teeny boy.

"I've never had a goose pie," he said. "And I'd really like to try a goose pie so maybe Daddy can kill the goose for us and you can make one of your famous pies with him, Mummy, and I'll put in my thumb and pull out one of his eyes and . . ."

I didn't hear any more. I was on my way home. It was clear to me that Little Jack Horner was not Georgie Porgie. His bottom was far too small.

When I got home, I found Spiffy the Sparrow waiting for me.

"I 'ear yer lookin' fer the one wot kissed all the girls," he said.

"That's right, Spiffy," I said. "His name's Georgie Porgie. Have you seen him?"

"Seen 'im?" echoed Spiffy. "Course I've seen 'im. Ev'ry time I looks in the mirror I sees 'im. Look no furver, Giddy. I'm yer Georgie Porgie."

"You kissed all the girls, Spiffy?" I cried. "But why?"

"Cos I like kissin' girls," said Spiffy.

"But you haven't got a big bottom, Spiffy," I said.

"I don't kiss girls wiv me bottom," said Spiffy.

"And you haven't got freckles or red hair or yellow shorts . . ."

"I c'n prove it was me," he said.

"How?" I asked.

"A nonentity parade," he said.

"What's that?" I asked.

"Yer line me up wiv a lot of uvver nonentities," he said, "an' then Bo-Peepy says which of us is Georgie Porgie."

It seemed a fair test. When Bo-Peep came home from school, I got Mother Goose and the goslings and Spiffy to stand in front of her – apart from Gary, who fell over in front of her – then I asked Bo-Peep to say which of them was Georgie Porgie.

She walked along the line, and when she came level with Spiffy, he jumped out, flew up, pecked her on the cheek, and said: "It's me, innit, darlin'?"

Bo-Peep shook her head.

"It's none of them," she said. "They don't look a bit like Georgie Porgie."

Yet again I had been proved right. Spiffy was not Georgie Porgie. Nor were Mother Goose and the goslings.

Spiffy shrugged his wing feathers.

"Win some, lose some," he said.

"Doesn't your friend the King eat pies?" asked Mother Goose.

It was true. One of my most famous cases concerned the nose that went missing after the King had had a pie with twenty-four blackbirds in it. The trouble with the King was that whenever I went to the palace, he always made me dig his garden, and I hate digging. Besides, if the King *was* Georgie Porgie, who was going to punish him? Anyone who pokes his head into the King's business is likely to find himself headless.

"No, my dear," I said to Mother Goose, "I know the King very well, and his bottom isn't big enough."

"The King isn't the only pie-eater in the palace," said Mother Goose.

She was right. As soon as she spoke, the idea occurred to me that Georgie Porgie could be someone else living in the palace. The King doesn't live there alone. The Queen, for instance, also lives there. She probably wouldn't dress up in yellow shorts and a spotty pink shirt and go round kissing girls, but what about the rest of the family, or the servants, or the servants' families? Gideon Gander was on the trail again.

I flew straight to the palace, and landed in the garden. I was just gazing at the scene of one of

my earlier triumphs – the burial place of Humpty
Dumpty – when who should come into the garden
but His Majesty himself.

"Hello," he said. "Goose, isn't it?"

"Gander, actually," I said, "but I'm honoured
that Your Majesty remembers me."

"Yes," he said. "Dig up the garden for me, will
you? Damn gardener's got 'flu. I'm off to do some
counting in the counting-house."

I hate digging. And I hate the King. No, I love
the King, because I've just remembered that the
King has the power to chop off heads. Hurray for
the King!

I spent the rest of the day digging the King's
garden. It was almost dark by the time he came
out to have a look.

"You still here, Goose?" he said. "Thought you'd
have finished long ago. What's that great pile of
weeds doing there?"

"I've just dug them up, Your Majesty," I said.

"Wouldn't have bothered if I were you," said
the King. "Of course the Queen's in charge of the
garden, but she's busy eating bread and pickle in

the parlour, along with our son George. He's eating pudding and pie. Never seen a boy eat so much. That's what gives him his fat tummy and his horrible breath and his freckles and his red cheeks and his red hair and his big bottom. Anyway, time you were going home, Goose, and I must go and do some counting. Take those weeds with you, will you?"

I wished I'd never gone to the palace. I found a big bag, put all the weeds in it, and dragged it off to the rubbish dump. Then I dragged myself off home.

"How did you get on?" asked Mother Goose.

I told her all about the King and the digging and the weeds.

"I've got aches," I said, "where I never even knew I had body."

"Did you see the Queen?" she asked.

"No," I said. "She was busy eating bread and pickle in the parlour, with her son George, who was eating pudding and pie."

"Pudding and pie?" repeated Mother Goose. "And his name is George? What does he look like?"

"I didn't see him either," I said. "And who cares what he looks like? Just ask me what I feel like!"

"I think," said Mother Goose, "you should go back to the palace tomorrow."

Mother Goose will never make a detective. I had presented her with all the right facts, and yet she had still drawn all the wrong conclusions.

"I am never going back there," I said. "He'll probably ask me to dig it all up again and replant his weeds."

"But you've got to see his son George," she said.

She clearly hadn't understood a word of what I'd said.

"What good will it do me," I asked, "to see Prince George eating pudding and pie?"

"Prince George," said Mother Goose, "sounds like the Georgie Porgie you're looking for."

It was at that moment that suddenly I began to put together all the information that I had collected that day. The name of the King's son was George, and the criminal was a Georgie Porgie. The King's son had been eating pudding and pie, and the criminal had left pudding and pie on the faces of the girls he'd kissed. And the King had said something about his son's fat tummy, horrible breath, freckles, red cheeks, red hair and big bottom, all of which were features of the criminal I was after. Unless I was much mistaken, I'd found my man.

The next day, I flew to the palace and landed in the garden.

"Ah, Goose, just the fellow I was looking for."

His Majesty the King was standing in front of me.

"The Queen wants you to dig up the garden again and put the weeds back in. She misses them. She'd tell you herself, but she's busy in the parlour eating bread and salami."

I uttered the loudest silent scream that has ever been unheard, and then I asked His Majesty where Prince George might be.

"Who?" he asked.

"Prince George," I repeated. "The one who was eating pudding and pie yesterday."

"Oh him," said the King. "Gone off to Switzerland. Can't keep him here – eats too much. Besides, he keeps rushing round kissing all the girls and making them cry. So we've sent him to boarding school, and good riddance, too. Now get on with that digging, will you? I've got some counting to do."

I should never have gone back to the palace. Not only was I now going to get aches on top of my aches, but also I wouldn't be able to see Prince George. Now we would never know whether or not he had been Georgie Porgie. Unless . . . perhaps there was still one possibility, a last chance for me to crack this case. I decided that whatever happened, I would take it.

I dragged myself off to the rubbish dump, found the bag of weeds, and dragged it and myself back to the palace. Then I spent the rest of the day digging and replanting the weeds I had dug up the previous day.

Night was falling when the King came out to have a look.

"Haven't you finished yet?" he asked.

"Not quite, Your Majesty," I said.

"Get a move on, then," he said. "I don't want

you here after dark. With that white coat of yours, everyone'll think you're a ghost."

It was now that I had to take my chance.

"May I ask you a question, Your Majesty?" I said.

It was a bold move, but courage has always been one of my braver characteristics.

"You already have," he said.

"Have I?" I asked.

"You asked if you could ask me a question," he said, "and that's a question. Well, hurry up with those weeds, Goose, and then honk off home. I must get on with some late-night counting."

"Your Majesty!" I cried. "Please let me ask one more question, so that I can die happy in your service."

"Well don't you die here," said the King. "Not unless you can bury yourself."

"I won't," I promised, "so long as Your Majesty will answer my question."

"What is it, then?" he asked.

This was the moment of truth.

"Your Majesty," I asked, "what was your son George wearing when he went to Switzerland?"

"I don't know," said the King. "But I expect it was his yellow shorts and spotty pink shirt as usual."

I had solved the mystery. With one simple question, I had put the final piece in the puzzle. If Prince George had been wearing anything else, I would have known that he was not Georgie Porgie, but he had been wearing yellow shorts and a spotty pink shirt, *and these were the very clothes Georgie Porgie had worn when he kissed the girls.* Thus I had proved that Prince George was in fact Georgie Porgie.

When I got home, I went straight into the Greens' living room.

"What is it, Gideon?" asked Mrs Green.

"I've solved the mystery of Georgie Porgie," I told her.

The whole family gathered round to hear the solution, and when I revealed the identity of the criminal there were gasps of astonishment. But there was one further twist to the story. Farmer Green was worried.

"If the King's son is the one having fun," he said, "what can be done?"

"Nothing to worry about," I said. "I've had him sent to Switzerland. He'll never bother us again."

It wasn't quite true that *I'd* sent him to Switzerland, but it gave the story a more impressive ending. And Gideon Gander is not only a master detective – he's also a master story-teller.

The Frightened Spider

The Case of the Frightened Spider was one of the most mysterious that I have ever tackled, and I doubt if any other detective in the world would have been clever enough to solve it. You will learn the facts as I learned them, and then you will shake your head in disbelief at the wondrous brain of the gander.

The story begins with one of Bo-Peep's friends, Little Miss Muffet. She was sitting on a tuffet eating her curds and whey, when a big spider came and sat down beside her. Understandably, Miss Muffet screamed and ran away as fast as her little legs could carry her. And since Mr Muffet had gone to work, and Mrs Muffet was looking after all the other Muffets, Little Miss Muffet ran to tell her friend Bo-Peep what had happened. At the time I was giving Gary a pecking lesson, but as soon as I heard the sobbing I hurried away to investigate.

Miss Muffet was upset not only because she was frightened of spiders, but also because she'd had to leave her curds and whey behind at the tuffet. This was already a bit of a mystery, because how anyone can like curds and whey I just don't know. Curds are solid sour milk, and whey is watery sour milk, but as far as I am concerned *any* sour milk is as yucky as pimples. If I'd been Miss Muffet, I'd have left my curds and whey as far behind as possible.

That, however, is not the mystery. Bo-Peep asked me if I'd go and chase the spider away so that Miss Muffet could get back to her dish of yuck. Now to tell you the truth, I don't much like spiders myself. In fact they have the same effect on me as curds and whey. One sight of all those straggly legs makes my feathers stand on end. I've seen spiders waving those twitchy legs round flies, covering them in shivery-shuddery, sticky-stucky threads, and I know that if I got anywhere near them, they'd do the same to me. For this reason I have always very sensibly stayed away from spiders. But if I'm asked for help, I don't like to refuse.

"Certainly," I said to Miss Muffet. "Nothing could be simpler. Just wait a moment, and I'll see if my wife would like to come along, too."

Mother Goose was quite surprised when I suggested that, since it was such a nice day, she and the goslings might join me on a little walk to the Muffets' place.

"Young Gary could do with a walking lesson," I said, "and I hear the Muffets have a lovely garden which you and the goslings will enjoy looking at."

Mother Goose was impressed. I don't often suggest taking the family out – or giving Gary lessons. I'm usually far too busy.

Off we all set, and I patiently showed Gary how to put the left leg forward, then the right leg, and then I picked him up and carried him. You can't teach Gary anything.

As we drew near the Muffets' garden, I called out in a loud voice, "Here we all come, then, to catch the nasty spider!"

If the spider had any sense, it would leg it to the nearest bush.

Miss Muffet pointed out her tuffet, which was right in the middle of a large lawn.

"Now then, Gary," I said, "let's just try once more. Left foot . . . right foot . . . "

Then I turned to Mother Goose.

"Perhaps, dear, while I'm seeing to Gary, you could just have a look if there's a spider on Miss Muffet's tuffet. I'll be with you in a minute."

To my relief, Mother Goose at once walked across to the tuffet. To my disappointment, she came back and said yes, there *was* a spider on Miss Muffet's tuffet. It was big hairy one, with lots of legs.

Little Miss Muffet screamed and clung to Bo-Peep.

"Right," I said. "We'll soon handle that. First, though, Mother Goose, could you . . . um . . . left foot, Gary, left, *left*, oops . . . could you . . . um . . . just see if Miss Muffet's dish of curds and whey is there?"

If I could get Mother Goose to go close enough to the tuffet, the spider was bound to see her and run away.

Back she came. There was a dish next to the tuffet, but it was empty.

"He's eaten all my curds and whey!" shrieked Miss Muffet.

"Spiders don't eat curds and whey," said Mother Goose. "Spiders eat flies."

It was an important point.

"That's an important point," I said. "We have a mystery on our hands. If the spider hasn't eaten the curds and whey, who has?"

If I could get them thinking about the mystery, they might forget about chasing away the spider.

"Maybe," said Bo-Peep, "Miss Muffet spilt the curds and whey on the grass when she ran away."

The same idea came into my head just a moment after Bo-Peep had said it.

"No," said Mother Goose, "there's nothing on the grass, and the dish is the right way up."

"If there's nothing on the grass," I said, "and the dish is the right way up, I don't think Miss Muffet could have spilt the curds and whey on the grass."

They all agreed with me.

"We therefore still have to solve the mystery," I said, "of who ate Miss Muffet's curds and whey."

"Never mind about that," sobbed Miss Muffet. "Go and chase the spider away."

It was a nasty moment.

"But . . . but we must find out who ate the curds and whey!" I protested.

"Perhaps the spider will tell us," said Mother Goose.

"Exactly," I said. "Exactly! We can't chase him away. He's our only witness."

"Then go and ask him who ate Miss Muffet's curds and whey," said Bo-Peep, "and then you can chase him away."

"I will," I said. "I certainly will. *I'm going to teach this spider a lesson he'll never forget!*"

I shouted that out really loud. Even a deaf spider would have heard it.

"But first, Miss Muffet," I said, "I want you to tell me the whole story, from start to finish. Then I shall know just what to ask the spider."

She told me that she had been sitting on a tuffet eating her curds and whey, when a big spider came and sat down beside her and frightened her away.

"Good," I said, "that confirms my suspicions."

"What suspicions?" she asked.

"That the spider hardy ardy mer mer woom," I said.

"Pardon?" she asked.

I hadn't been able to think of anything else to say.

"You'd better go and question the spider, Gideon," said Mother Goose.

"In a moment," I said. "In just one moment. But first I have one more very important question to ask. A very, very important question. A very, very, very important question."

"What is it?" asked Miss Muffet.

I didn't know. But somehow I had to keep this conversation going.

"When did you first see the spider?" I asked.

Actually it wasn't a bad question.

"He came dangling down next to my ear," said Miss Muffet.

"Ah!" I said. "Which ear?"

She pointed to her left ear.

"Good," I said. "It's all getting clearer."

"That's strange," said Mother Goose.

"What's strange?" I asked. I was making a good job of this conversation.

"If the spider dangled down next to your ear," said Mother Goose to Miss Muffet, "where did it come from?"

I'm afraid Mother Goose will never make a good detective. I was glad that she was asking questions, but this was a very silly one.

"Spiders, my dear," I said, "come from webs. Everyone knows that."

"But where would the web have been?" asked Mother Goose.

"On a bush or up a tree," I said. "Spiders make their webs everywhere."

I have in fact made quite a study of spiders, and am able to speak with some authority.

"But the tuffet's in the middle of the lawn," said Mother Goose. "And there are no bushes or trees there. So when the spider dangled down, what did he dangle down from?"

I looked at Mother Goose, and I looked at the tuffet, and I looked above the tuffet. She was right. There was nothing above the tuffet except empty sky. Slowly an idea began to form in my mind. If the spider had come down from above the tuffet, he could not have come from a web, since not even a clever spider can build a web in mid air. And in that case, we now had two mysteries on our hands: who had eaten the curds and whey, and where had the spider come from?

"There's an easy way to find out," said Mother Goose.

I certainly couldn't see it, but was eager to hear what it was.

"Ask the spider," said Mother Goose.

I should not have been so eager.

"Go and ask him, Giddy," said Bo-Peep, "and then chase him away so that Miss Muffet can sit on her tuffet again."

"I don't think I shall ever want to sit there again," said Miss Muffet.

"Oh well," I said, "in that case there isn't much point in me — "

"Go and solve the mystery, dear," said Mother Goose, "or do you want me to do it?"

"No, no, absolutely not," I said. "This is my job. But . . . um . . . you can come with me if you like."

She did. In fact, she even walked on ahead of me. This may have been because I was walking rather slowly. She reached the tuffet, and then to my surprise just stood there shaking her head.

"Gone, has he?" I called out. "Damn!"

"No, he's still here," she said.

"Ugh, oh, good," I said.

"But I've never seen a spider like this one," said Mother Goose. "Come and have a look, Gideon."

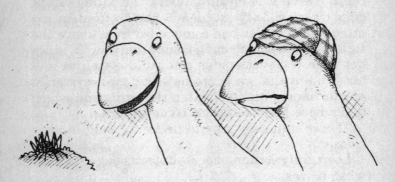

I drew myself up to my full height, and swaggered across to the tuffet. There he was — fat, hairy, with ten thousand legs ... but Mother Goose was right. There was something very strange about him. He was trembling all over — not leg-waving, sticky-spinny trembling, but jelly-wobbling, scared-stiff trembling.

"What's wrong with him?" I asked.

"Spider, what's wrong with you?" asked Mother Goose.

The spider said nothing. He just went on trembling.

"He's probably scared of us," I said.

It was a good theory. I'm a pretty impressive figure. Even a huge and hairy spider like that one would tremble at what I might do to him if I was ever foolish enough to come close.

"If he was scared of us," said Mother Goose, "he'd have run away long ago. No, this spider's in a state of shock. He's too frightened even to talk."

"In that case," I said, "let's go home and forget the whole thing."

"But I'd really like to know where he came from," said Mother Goose, "and who ate the curds and whey."

"We could leave him our address," I said, "and ask him to contact us when he's recovered."

"I've got a better idea," she said. "I'll fetch Doctor Foster to have a look at him. But we'd better move him first, so that Miss Muffet can have her tuffet back."

"Right!" I said. "If you move the spider, I'll let Miss Muffet know what we're doing."

Off I rushed. When I looked back, I saw Mother Goose lean over, pick the spider up in her beak, and carry it into the bushes at the side of the garden. I would have to remember not to kiss her goodnight.

I went across to where Bo-Peep and Miss Muffet were standing.

"We've shifted the spider," I said to Miss Muffet. "He won't bother you any more."

"Thank you, Gideon," she said.

"It was nothing," I replied.

"Did you find out where he came from and who ate the curds and whey?" asked Bo-Peep.

"No," I said, "but I have an idea."

The idea that I had was that I would go and accuse Wolfie. He may have had nothing to do with the crime, but if I waited in the Muffets' garden for Doctor Foster, Gary was sure to need a lesson in something.

I told Mother Goose where I was going.

"Wolves don't eat curds and whey," she remarked.

"You said the same about spiders," I replied, "but look what happened."

"What happened?" she asked.

"The spider handy andy wam pam rubbished," I said, and flew off to interrogate Wolfie.

"Hot on another cold trail, eh, Goosey?" sneered Wolfie as soon as he saw me.

"You can sneer, Wolfie," I said, "but I'll catch you one day."

"Not before I catch you," said Wolfie. "Now then, what am I supposed to have done today?"

"You frightened Miss Muffet," I said, "and ate her curds and whey."

"Curds and whey?" echoed Wolfie. "No one in their right mind eats curds and whey!"

"Exactly!" I said. "And that's how I know you did it."

It was one of the cleverest replies I have ever

heard. I repeated it three times, to make sure Wolfie had understood what I meant.

"You get it, Wolfie?" I asked.

"I get it," said Wolfie. "What there is of it. But I didn't get your curds and whey. I don't eat curds and whey. I eat geese."

"There's no need to be rude," I said. "Well, if you didn't do it, who did?"

"You're the detective," he replied. "Find out."

"I intend to," I said.

I was winning this argument comfortably.

"One last question," I said. "What frightened the spider?"

"Oh good, a riddle," said Wolfie. "I don't know. What did frighten the spider?"

"It's not a riddle," I answered.

"Yes it is," he said. "I'll ask you, then. I say, I say, I say, what frightened the spider?"

"I don't know," I replied. "What did frighten the spider?"

"The terri-fly," said Wolfie.

It didn't seem very funny to me, but Wolfie howled with laughter, and I left him lying on the ground waving his legs in the air.

I flew straight back to the Muffets' garden, hoping that by now Doctor Foster would have solved the mystery and saved me a lot of trouble. When I arrived, he was kneeling by the red-currant bush in his underpants, with his stethoscope to his ears. Mother Goose and the goslings were standing round him, while Bo-Peep and Miss Muffet stood on the other side of the lawn.

"Why is he in his underpants?" I asked Mother Goose.

"He's just come from Gloucester," she said, "and while he was there, he stepped into a puddle which went right up to his middle, so his trousers got wet."

"Shh!" hissed the Doctor. "I'm trying to listen!"

"What's he listening to?" I whispered to Mother Goose.

"The spider's heart," she whispered back.

We all waited in silence, and at last the doctor straightened up.

"The chocolaxic tube is defrigerated, the odiferous ping-pung is perfumigated, and the radiatory gasket has been carburettored," he said.

"I see," I said. "How is he, then?"

"Dead," said the Doctor.

I can't say I was sorry. On the other hand, death is a serious business, and I didn't want the Doctor to think I hadn't understood what it meant.

"Oh no!" I cried. "Dead? Poor spider! What a tragedy!"

"I thought you didn't like spiders," said Mother Goose.

"I had grown fond of this one," I said. "And, after all, death is so final, is it not, Doctor?"

I think he was quite impressed with my grasp of the medical facts.

Just then Spoffy the Sparrow, brother to Spiffy, flew into the garden.

"Fank 'eavens I found you 'ere!" he said to the Doctor. "Come quick, will yer? Me bruvver's bin took ill."

"Not another illness," grumbled the Doctor. "I'm sick of all these sicknesses. At this rate I'll

51

never get my trousers back on. What's the matter with your brother?"

"I dunno," said Spoffy. "If I knoo wot was the matter wiv 'im, I wouldn' 'ave ter call you, would I?"

"Everyone's always calling me!" moaned Doctor Foster. "Never want to see me when they're well. Just keep calling me when they're ill."

Grumbling all the time, he put his stethoscope in his bag.

"One moment, Doctor," I said. "Aren't you supposed to leave a prescription for the patient?"

"Certainly," he said. "Take one hole, put it in the ground, and bury him in it."

I was still no nearer to solving the mystery. What I was nearer to was going home, which meant another walking or being-carried lesson for Gary.

"I think I'd better go with Doctor Foster," I told Mother Goose. "I'm worried about Spiffy. He may need my help. If you just give Gary his walking lesson, I'll get home as quickly as I can."

I rushed off at once, not wanting poor Spiffy to suffer for a moment longer than necessary. Spoffy and the Doctor followed on behind me.

Spiffy really was suffering. He was rolling on the ground hugging his stomach with his wings and groaning quite pitifully.

"Well?" asked the Doctor. "What seems to be the trouble?"

"It's me tum!" cried Spiffy. "Oooh, aaah, wot a pain, wot a belly-ache!"

"Agonistes in the abdopuff, is it?" said the Doctor. "What have you been eating?"

"I dunno!" said Spiffy, rolling sideways, front-

ways and backways in his agony.

"Keep still, you silly sparrow," said the Doctor. "I can't examine you here if you're over there."

He gave Spiffy a poke and a prod, a pull and a push, and a pinch and a punch.

"Ow!" said Spiffy.

"Well," said the Doctor, "the spiracocks are in order, and the tittibonks. Any pain in the algebrax?"

"The wot?"

"Turn over ... stand up ... sit down ... bend ... stretch ... flap your right wing ... flap your left wing ... stand up ... raise your right leg ... raise your left leg ... raise both legs ... " (At this Spiffy fell flat on his back.)

"Is this doin' 'im any good, Doctor?" asked Spoffy.

"No," said the Doctor, "but *I'm* enjoying it."

What happened next was very interesting. After all these uppings and downings, Spiffy was very, very sick. He yucked up whatever he'd been eating, and whatever he'd been eating was all white and curdly.

53

"Just as I thought," said the Doctor. "Curds and whey. You'll feel better now you've got rid of it. Everyone feels better when they've got rid of their curds and whey. Don't eat it again. And call me any time, so long as you're not ill. I've had enough of patients who are ill. From now on, I'm only going to treat patients who are well."

He left Spiffy, Spoffy and me all gazing at Spiffy's curds and whey. And as we gazed at them, an idea slowly began to form in my mind.

"Spiffy," I said, "where did you *get* the curds and whey?"

"I gorrit from Miss Muffet," said Spiffy, "an' I don't arf wish I 'adn't."

"How did you 'get it from her?" I asked.

"Well," he said, "she's scared stiff o' spiders. So I picked up this spider in me beak, see, flew over Miss Muffet, an' dropped 'im right beside 'er. She screamed an' run away, leavin' 'er curds an' whey be'ind. Then I 'ad it all ter meself, worse luck."

There was one more vital question to be asked. I gave Spiffy a deeply penetrating look.

"I want the truth now, Spiffy," I said. "Think carefully. What did the spider say when you picked him up and dropped him?"

"'E never said nuffin'," Spiffy replied. "'E was even more scared than Miss Muffet."

The case of the frightened spider shows how a superdetective can find a solution from details that anyone else would certainly overlook. Perhaps you have not even worked out the solution yet yourself.

The Doctor had identified Spiffy's yuck as curds and whey. Miss Muffet's curds and whey had been stolen. That meant that Spiffy could have been the thief. Then Spiffy said he had dropped a spider next to Miss Muffet, and at once I realized that there might be a link between *that* spider and the spider I had seen on Miss Muffet's tuffet. But my most brilliant piece of detection had been my final question. This was the question that cracked the case. If Spiffy had reported that his spider had said something, I'd have known that he was lying. But the spider had been too scared to say anything. And the spider on the tuffet had also been too scared to say anything. That proved, beyond any doubt, that Spiffy's spider and the spider on Miss Muffet's tuffet were one and the same spider! That's what I call detective work.

When I got home, I asked Mother Goose how Gary's walking lesson had gone. Then I asked her what she thought of Miss Muffet's garden, and what were her views on spiders, and whether she thought we should feed Gary on curds and whey. I think she was a little puzzled at this conversation. But then, after a few more minutes, I casually said to her, "Oh, by the way, I've solved the mystery of where the spider came from, and who ate the curds and whey."

When I told her, she was really impressed. And

so was Bo-Peep. And so was Miss Muffet. And so was everybody else I told, and I told everybody else I knew.

Even Wolfie was impressed, and had to agree that it had been an unusual case.

"*You* solved the crime?" he asked.

"I certainly did," I confirmed.

"Well, that sure is unusual," said Wolfie.

The Missing Dog

Bo-Peep had been given a little dog named Sweetheart. The Muffets gave it to her as a thank you present for helping Miss Muffet get over the spider shock. It's my belief that they gave it to her because they wanted to get rid of it. That dog was the biggest pain since Humpty Dumpty fell off the wall. If I had to choose between an hour with Gary Gosling and five minutes with Sweetheart, I'd take the hour with Gary.

He was a tiny creature with long white hair, a short tail, long ears, and a red ribbon tied round his neck. All day long he would bounce around telling everyone how wuff wuff wonderful he was, how yap yap happy we should all be to know him, and how grrr grrr grrreat the world would be if only it were full of Sweethearts. He was a Little Jack Horner on four legs.

He also had sharp little teeth which he kept nipping us with. Not a leg, wing or bottom was safe from those little razors, but if you so much as raised a foot in self-defence, he'd go running to the Greens. For some reason which even the world's greatest detective could never discover, the Greens loved that dog. They'd pet him and hug him and cuddle him, and the monster would nestle in their arms and act as if marrowbone jelly wouldn't melt in his mouth.

"Did the nasty goosey-woosey twy to kick poor lickle Sweetypie, then?" Bo-Peep would say, as I limped away on legs covered with toothmarks.

"Yap yap yes!" cried Sweetheart.

"Shall Bo-Peep give him a smacky?"

"Give him a woof woof whipping!"

Then I'd get a smack just where I'd been bitten, and he'd get a kiss just where I'd like to have given him a punch.

I'll give you one example of this evil creature's behaviour. One day, I happened to wander into the kitchen. I often wander into the kitchen, and some of my most famous cases have begun there. You'll recall that it was the kitchen where I first met Mrs Grundy. Another reason why I wander into the kitchen is that there might be something tasty lying around, and I happen to be fond of tasty things.

On this particular day, I noticed a bunch of asparagus lying on the table. Now I love asparagus. I'd give a dozen hot cross buns just for one spear of asparagus, and seeing a whole bunch of them was like walking into paradise. There was no one around. In any case, after all the mysteries I'd solved for the Greens, a spear or two of asparagus was the least they could give me in return. As it happened, I ate rather more than a spear or two. The trouble with asparagus is, once you start, it's difficult to stop. One more spear, one more spear, I kept saying to myself. So I ate one more spear until there were no more spears.

"Wuff wuff wuff I saw you, I saw you!" came the dreaded voice, and there in the kitchen doorway stood the Nuisance of the Yard.

"I saw you, Gideon, I saw you, and I'm going to tell the grrr grrr Grrreens that you ate their asparagus bark bark barkause that's stealing and you're not supposed to steal!"

Off he rushed to find Mrs Green, and off I

rushed to find a hiding-place. I found a good one, too – in the long grass round the back of the barn. They'd never find me there . . . so I thought. But I'd reckoned without the sneaky, snoopy sniffiness of Sweetheart's nose. He followed my trail all the way from the kitchen. And Mrs Green accompanied Sweetheart, and the broomhandle accompanied Mrs Green.

"There he is, Mrs grrr grrr Grrreen," wuffed the abominable tell-tale, "in the long grrr grrr grrrass at the bark bark back of the bark bark barn!"

Then he came plunging towards me, and nipped me in a part of the body that should never be nipped. I let out a huge honk of agony, and ran for my life.

Another honk of agony followed a bonk of broomstick. It was all so unfair. Case after case I've solved for the Greens, and I protect them from burglars, murderers, and Wolfie, yet I got a broomhandling while Sweetheart – who never solved a case in his life – got kisses and cuddles.

But the blame wasn't entirely Mrs Green's. Even in the midst of my suffering, my detective's brain was weighing up the facts. There was no doubt at all in my mind that the really guilty party was Sweetheart. If Sweetheart hadn't seen me eating the asparagus, and if Sweetheart hadn't told Mrs Green that I'd eaten it, and if Sweetheart hadn't nosed my trail into the long grass at the back of the barn, I'd never have been broomhandled.

Two days later, Sweetheart disappeared. I heard the news when I wandered into the kitchen and found Johnny and Bo-Peep in tears, Mrs Green looking grave, and Farmer Green looking grim.

"Oh where, oh where has my little dog gone? Oh where, oh where can he be?" sobbed Bo-Peep.

"We don't know, darling," said Mrs Green, "but we'll find him."

"And when the hound has been found," said Farmer Green, "I'll clobber the robber."

It was clearly a case for Gideon Gander.

"Oh please find him, Gideon!" cried Little Bo-Peep. "I love him so much!"

It would have been nice if she'd said she loved me, too. In fact it was noble of me to take the case at all after what Sweetheart had done to me.

Sweetheart had last been seen the night before, when he had gone to bed in his special, fur-lined basket in the hall. In the morning, he had simply vanished, and the only clue was that the kitchen door was open. Now almost anyone can open the kitchen door if they know how to nudge the latch. I can open it myself. But Sweetheart was too small to reach it, and so obviously someone had crept in during the night and taken him away. The only question was: who?

I walked across the yard to the barn to have a word with Tozer, our watchdog. He's so old and lazy that he keeps watch with his eyes closed, but I thought he might have heard something.

"Ugh ugh!" yawned Tozer. "What, ugh, some-one stole Sweetheart? Good. Useless noisy animal, always waking me up to tell me I ought to be awake. Good riddance, I say."

I said the same thing, but I said it to myself.

"Did you see or hear anything in the night, Tozer?" I asked.

"Absolutely nothing," he said.

I knew why he'd seen and heard nothing. He'd been fast asleep.

"Well done, Tozer," I said.

Doodle the Cock and Pussy and the kittens had all been fast asleep as well. I called round at the Muffets, in case Sweetheart had been taken back there, but Little Miss Muffet hadn't seen him; nor had Mr and Mrs Muffet.

"Who would want to harm such a sweet little dog?" asked Mrs Muffet.

"It's unbelievable, isn't it?" I said. "We're all heartbroken."

On my way home from the Muffets, I met Spiffy the Sparrow. Spiffy is a known criminal — you will recall that I caught him stealing Miss Muffet's curds and whey — and more than once I've got him to confess to crimes. It would save me a lot of work if he confessed to this one.

"I 'ear Sweet'eart's gorn missin'," he said.

"Where have you taken him, Spiffy?" I asked.

"Never touched 'im," said Spiffy. "Not me, mate. Got nuffink ter do wiv me."

That was a disappointment.

"Do you mean you're not going to confess, Spiffy?" I asked.

"I ain't confessin'," said Spiffy, "to a crime for which Farmer Green is goin' ter clobber the robber."

"Can you prove you didn't do it?" I asked.

"I can," he said. " 'Ave I bin clobbered?"

"No," I said.

"Well," he said, "if Farmer Green is goin' ter clobber the robber, an' I ain't bin clobbered, I can't be the robber, can I?"

He was right.

"Then if you didn't do it, Spiffy," I asked, "who did?"

"Wolfie," he said.

It's a remarkable fact that whenever a crime is committed, everyone suspects Wolfie (or Spiffy). I have often suspected him myself. But it seemed to me that in this case, there were good reasons why Wolfie should not be questioned.

"Nonsense, Spiffy," I said. "Wolfie wouldn't dare come to the Greens' farm, let alone go into their house. He couldn't even have known where to find Sweetheart. No, Spiffy, this is one case where we can leave Wolfie in peace."

"Well if I was a detective," said Spiffy, "I'd go an' queschun Wolfie."

"But you're not a detective, Spiffy," I said. "I am."

He couldn't argue with that.

By now we were back at the yard, and Bo-Peep had overheard the last part of our conversation.

"I agree with Spiffy," she said. "It's Wolfie who's taken my darling Sweetheart, it is, I know it is. Go and question him, Gideon, and get my little dog back from him. Please."

I couldn't say no to Bo-Peep. Off I flew to Wolfie's, and Spiffy came with me. I told him it might be dangerous, but he insisted on coming. I think he enjoyed watching the masterbrain at work.

"Hello, Wolfie," I said.

It was a way of putting him at his ease.

"Hello, Goosey," he said.

I ignored the mistake. It's never easy to interrogate Wolfie, but this time it was especially difficult. I needed to phrase my questions very carefully.

"You didn't steal Sweetheart, did you?" I said.

"No," he said.

His answer was exactly what I had expected.

"There you are," I said to Spiffy. "Wolfie's not guilty."

"Oh?" said Spiffy. "Then wot's that red ribbon doin' on the ground beside 'im?"

Spiffy was right. There *was* a red ribbon next to Wolfie.

"I bought it from Simple Simon," said Wolfie.

"Ah!" I said. "That explains it."

"Sweet'eart 'ad a red ribbon like that," said Spiffy.

"Did he?" I asked.

"An' I reckon that's Sweet'eart's red ribbon on the ground next ter Wolfie," said Spiffy.

I was beginning to find Spiffy's help annoying.

"Now look here, Spiffy," I said, "who's the detective, you or me?"

"You're the detective," he said, "an' Wolfie's the criminal, an' Sweet'eart's the victim."

"We'll soon see about that," I said. "Wolfie, are you the criminal?"

"No," said Wolfie.

"There you are, Spiffy," I said. "You can't have a clearer statement than that."

"Yer can't 'ave a clearer lie than that," said Spiffy. "Let's go an' ask Simple Simon if 'e sold Wolfie a red ribbon."

I didn't like the way Spiffy was taking charge of this case. Hadn't I already proved that Wolfie couldn't have done it? I apologized to Wolfie.

"That's all right, Goosey," he said. "So long as *you* believe in me."

I found his faith quite touching.

"Nothing for sale!" cried Simple Simon. "Nothing for sale! Come and buy my nothing!"

"How much is it?" I asked.

"How much do you want?" he asked.

"Well, none of it, really," I said.

"In that case," he said, "it won't cost you anything."

"Ask 'im about the ribbon," said Spiffy.

I asked Simple Simon when he had sold the red ribbon to Wolfie. He sat there for a few minutes, and then said that he couldn't remember. I asked him who he'd got the red ribbon from, and again he sat there for a few minutes, and again he said he couldn't remember.

"It sounds pretty suspicious to me," I said to Spiffy.

"Why can't yer remember?" Spiffy asked Simple Simon.

"Because I can't remember a red ribbon," said Simple Simon.

"That proves it!" said Spiffy. " 'E never sold a red ribbon ter Wolfie. Wolfie got it off Sweet'eart when 'e ate 'im!"

We flew straight back to Wolfie's, and Spiffy accused him of taking the red ribbon off Sweetheart when he ate him.

"What red ribbon?" said Wolfie.

It was a surprising twist in the case. There was no sign of a red ribbon anywhere.

" 'E's 'idden it!" said Spiffy.

"Hidden what?" said Wolfie.

"The red ribbon," said Spiffy.

"What red ribbon?" said Wolfie again.

Clearly this conversation was going round in circles. The fact was that the red ribbon had disappeared just like Sweetheart himself. And without the red ribbon, it was impossible to connect Wolfie with the crime. Now, in this country, a Wolfie is innocent until proved guilty, and no matter what Spiffy said, I was not prepared to go round accusing an innocent criminal unless I had proof.

"It's no good, Spiffy," I said. "If Wolfie says he's innocent, then he's innocent."

" 'E's guilty," said Spiffy.

"One for, one against," said Wolfie. "In that case, I get the casting vote, and I say Wolfie's innocent."

That made it two-to-one in Wolfie's favour, and although Spiffy said it wasn't a fair vote, Wolfie and I agreed that the case was closed. I flew back to the yard.

"Was it Wolfie?" asked Bo-Peep. "Has he given Sweetheart back to you?"

"No," I said, "it wasn't Wolfie, and alas our beloved Sweetheart is nowhere to be found. I'm sorry, Bo-Peep."

Her little face crumpled like the horn of one of

Farmer Green's cows. It was a sad day. Bo-Peep had lost her dog, and, for the first time in history, Gideon Gander had failed to solve a mystery.

Sweetheart was never seen again. But a few weeks later, Bo-Peep was given another dog – a much nicer one, called Yum-Yum – and everyone lived happily ever after. Except Sweetheart.

You will have been shocked, though, to hear that the world's greatest detective had failed to solve the mystery. The time has now come to set the record straight. I did solve it. In fact, there never was a mystery. Spiffy was right – in spite of the two-to-one vote, Wolfie was guilty. Wolfie knew it, and I knew it. We also knew who it was that invited Wolfie to the Greens' house at dead of night, opened the kitchen door for him, and showed him the way to Sweetheart's fur-lined basket in the hall. But I'm not going to tell you who that was.

Lucy Lurse's Purse

Bo-Peep had invited two of her schoolfriends to play with her: Lucy Lurse and Kitty Fisher. Three little girls playing happily in the yard really shouldn't have caused any problems, but they did. First there was a loss, which was bad enough, and then there was a crime, which was even wocket.

You may not know what I mean when I say "wocket". Well, wocket means worse. And worse means wocket. And Lucy Lurse was actually Lucy Locket, or maybe Lucy Locket was Lucy Lurse. It's all very confusing.

"Let's play nockets!" Lucy cried to the other girls.

"What are nockets?" asked Bo-Peep.

"She means nurses," said Kitty Fisher.

So Lucy was the patient, Kitty was the nurse, and Bo-Peep was the doctor.

"Are you feeling better?" asked Bo-Peep.

"No," said Lucy. "Just the revocket. I'm wocket."

It sounded like a foreign language to me.

But the real trouble came later when I heard screams from behind the barn where the girls had gone to play hide-and-seek. I rushed across and found Lucy in tears.

"What's the matter?" I asked.

"I've lost my pocket," sobbed Lucy.

"Lost your pocket?" I said. "But you've still got your pocket. Look! On your dress."

"No!" she cried. "My pocket! My pocket! It was in my purse, and now it's gone!"

"Your pocket was in your purse?" I said.

"She means her purse was in her pocket," said Kitty Fisher. "She gets her 'urses' and her 'ockets' mixed up."

"So what has she lost?" I asked.

"Her purse," said Kitty.

"Very well," I said, "we must look for it."

I have always found that when something is lost, the best way to find it is to look for it. But you can save a lot of time if you know *where* to look for it.

"Where exactly did you lose it?" I asked.

"I don't know," said Lucy.

That didn't tell us much, but Lucy wasn't too good at telling things anyway.

"When did you last see it?" asked Bo-Peep.

"When we were playing nockets," said Lucy.

"You mean nurses," I said.

"That's right," she said. "Nockets."

There was something about her that reminded me of Gary the Gosling.

We were all standing behind the barn, and suddenly I remembered another occasion when something had been lying in the grass and had then been found. Me. You will recall when poor little Sweetheart – such a loss to us all – had come looking for me in order to betray me to Mrs Green. As I discovered that day, dogs are good at finding things.

"Don't worry, Lucy," I said. "I'll soon find your purse."

I walked into the barn, which is where Tozer the watchdog sleeps day and night.

"Wake up, Tozer," I said. "We've got a job for you."

71

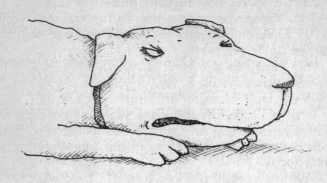

He opened one eye.

"And I've got a job for you," he said.

"What's that?" I asked.

"Make sure nobody wakes me up," he said, and closed his eye.

"You've got to find Lucy's purse!" I honked in his ear.

"Find it yourself," he yawned.

Once more I remembered the dear departed Sweetheart, and the clever little trick he would use to make us do things for him.

"If you don't go and find Lucy's purse," I said, "I'll tell Farmer Green."

Tozer opened both eyes. My words had struck home.

"Ugh ugh," he said. "Aren't you supposed to be a great detective?"

"I *am* a great detective," I said.

"Well go and tell Farmer Green that the great detective couldn't even find a purse."

He was right. A great detective ought to be able to find a purse. If I let Tozer find it, he'd claim that *he* had solved the case.

"You'd better stay there, Tozer," I said. "Leave this to me."

"I wouldn't dream of doing anything else," he said, and closed his eyes again.

Just at that moment, Kitty Fisher's voice sounded out from behind the barn: "I've found it! Look, everybody, I've found it!"

I rushed out, and there she stood in the long grass with a purse in her hand. It was a little brown purse tied up with a piece of red ribbon. Along came Lucy.

"That's it!" she cried. "It's my pocket, you've found my pocket!"

But then she looked puzzled.

"What's that ribbon doing round my pocket?" she asked.

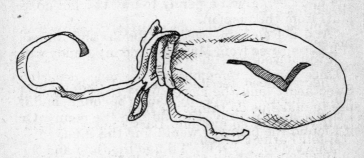

"Wasn't it there before?" I asked.

"No," she said.

She untied the ribbon, opened the purse, and screamed.

"What's the matter now?" I asked.

"My penny!" she cried. "My penny's gone!"

I turned to Kitty.

"What does she mean?" I asked.

Kitty gave me a funny look.

"She means her penny's gone," she said.

"Who's stolen my penny?" cried Lucy.

I quickly worked out that Lucy must have had a penny in her purse, and now it was missing. And if the penny had been stolen, as she claimed, there must be a thief around. The case was becoming complicated.

"Are you sure you had a penny in it?" asked Bo-Peep.

I listened carefully to the reply. I needed to, if I was going to understand it.

"Yes," said Lucy.

I understood it. It meant that she had had a penny in her purse. She went on to explain that she had been given a penny to buy two hot cross buns from the pieman.

"And if I go home without them," she wailed, "I'll get a rurse from Mummy, and my Daddy will cocket me."

That sounded terrible, even if I didn't know what it meant. The penny had to be found, and if I could find the thief, I would find the penny. Or if I found the penny, I would find the thief.

"Don't worry," I said. "I'll find the thief and the penny. And the penny and the thief."

They were brave words.

"I wonder who tied the ribbon round the purse," said Bo-Peep.

It was my first clue. I had already established that the ribbon had not been there before, and so it was possible that whoever had tied the ribbon had stolen the penny.

"That's what I want to know," I said. "Who tied the ribbon?"

"Me," said a familiar voice from out of the long grass.

It was Spiffy.

"You, Spiffy?" I asked.

"Course it was me," said Spiffy. "I tied it wiv me beak, didn't I?"

"I see. In that case, Spiffy," I said, "you must be the thief."

"I confess," said Spiffy.

"Then give it back to Lucy at once!" said Bo-Peep.

"I 'ave," replied Spiffy.

Lucy said he hadn't, Spiffy said he had, and so Lucy looked in her purse/pocket and her pockets/purses, and said it wasn't there.

"Course it's there," said Spiffy. "Yer 'oldin' it in yer 'and."

But apart from her purse, all Lucy had in her hand was the ribbon.

"Give her back the penny!" said Bo-Peep.

"Wot penny?" asked Spiffy.

"The penny that was stolen," said Bo-Peep.

"I fought you said it was a ribbon," said Spiffy.

I had listened carefully to this conversation, and swiftly worked out what it meant. Spiffy knew nothing about the penny. He thought we were talking about the ribbon. And so the case had taken another unexpected turn.

"All right, Spiffy," I said, "you'd better tell me where you stole the ribbon from."

"Let's 'ave a good look," he said.

Lucy showed him the ribbon.

"Red, eh?" he said. "Well, I got that from Wolfie, didn't I? That's the ribbon wot was tied round that little dog wot Wolfie ... "

It was a nasty moment. He was about to give away the most closely guarded secret of my whole career.

"Nonsense!" I said. "Sheer nonsense, Spiffy! How can you talk such nonsense? Wolfie would never let you steal the ribbon he ties round his little log. Wolfie guards his little log night and and day. You're telling lies again, aren't you, Spiffy? I'm sorry, Lucy. I'm sorry, Bo-Peep. Spiffy clearly knows nothing about this ribbon."

"What's more to the point," said Bo-Peep, "he clearly knows nothing about Lucy's penny."

"Exactly," I said. "We're looking for a penny, not a ribbon, so stop talking about ribbons, Spiffy, will you?"

I had dealt very cleverly with a difficult situation, and yet for some reason Lucy and Bo-Peep were still unhappy. In fact, Lucy was crying harder than ever.

"I want my penny back," she sobbed.

"Come on, Gideon," said Bo-Peep, "stop wasting time with Spiffy and find Lucy's penny."

It was easy enough for her to say. But if Spiffy hadn't got the penny, who had? Even Gideon Gander can't just produce a thief and a penny out of nowhere.

"Maybe the penny's 'idin' in the grass," said Spiffy.

This gave me an idea.

"Maybe," I said, "the thief is hiding in the grass. Come on out, you penny thief! I can see you!"

Nobody came out.

"Come on out, you penny!" shouted Spiffy. "I can see yer!"

The penny didn't come out either. I looked at the faces of the three little girls – all waiting for me to do something. Then I looked at Spiffy. And I looked at the long grass, looked at the barn, looked up at the sky, looked round the Greens' house . . . There was nothing else for me to do except look.

"What is it, Gideon?" asked Bo-Peep. "Have you found a clue?"

I was, of course, clueless, but I have my reputation to think of.

"Yes" I said.

"What is it?" she asked.

"I can't tell you yet," I said, and that was certainly true. "But I need some help." That was true, too.

"What sort of help?" she asked.

The sort of help I needed was somebody saying: "I did it, and here's the penny." But such help never comes when you want it, except from Spiffy, and that doesn't count.

"The sort of help I need," I said, "is agrabartographical."

"What?" she asked.

"It's a technical term," I said, "used by detectives."

"He's never going to find my penny!" wailed Lucy.

"Yes he is," said Bo-Peep. "You will find it, won't you, Gideon?"

"Of course I will," I said.

I only wished I knew how. They were all looking at me.

"Now listen carefully," I said.

They listened carefully. All I needed now was something to say.

"The facts are these," I said. "Lucy has lost her purse with a penny in it. Now it's been found without its penny, tied up with a piece of ribbon that we can forget about. These are the facts. Now think hard. Can you see the connection between those facts, and from the connection can you work out the identity of the thief? Or the whereabouts of the penny?"

I was just hoping that one of them would come up with an answer. They all thought hard.

"It was me," said Spiffy.

"No it wasn't," I said.

"Then, if it wasn't me," said Spiffy, "it was someone else."

He was right.

"Do *you* know who it was, Gideon?" asked Bo-Peep.

"Yes, of course," I said. What else could I say? A detective is supposed to know these things.

Now this was the moment at which something very strange happened. Kitty Fisher's face turned red. Until then it had just been an ordinary whitish pink, but now it had become as red as a piece of ribbon.

"Do . . . do you really kn . . . know who it is?" she asked.

"Yes," I said. Having said yes once, I could hardly say no now.

Then Kitty began to cry, and through the tears that fell down her red cheeks, she said something that I found very interesting.

"I did it!" she sobbed. "I took the penny!"

It was a great moment. I pointed a wing straight at Kitty, and cried, "Kitty is the thief!"

At the same time, she took a bright shiny penny out of her pocket.

"And that," I cried, "is the penny that Kitty stole from Lucy's purse!"

Everybody gasped. Gideon Gander had triumphed again. I ordered Kitty to tell us the full story, but she couldn't speak through her sobs.

"Very well," I said. "I'll tell you all the full story myself."

I didn't know it, but it was easy enough to guess.

"Lucy dropped her purse in the long grass," I said, "and Kitty found it. Am I right, Kitty?"

She nodded.

"She took out the penny, then dropped the purse again. Spiffy came along with his piece of ribbon, tied the purse up — "

"No I never," said Spiffy. "I never 'ad nuffink ter do wiv it. I was fibbin'."

"Exactly!" I said. "Just as I thought. Yet again, Spiffy, I've proved what a fibber you are."

He had already admitted he was a fibber, and so yet again I was right. But I was still a little puzzled about where the ribbon had come from. Eventually Kitty stopped crying and admitted that she had taken the ribbon from her hair and tied the purse up with it. She'd hoped that this would stop Lucy from opening the purse. She said she was very sorry, and would never do it again, and so Lucy forgave her and the girls went off to play find-the-pocket. I turned to my old friend Spiffy.

"There you are, Spiffy," I said. "Another mystery solved."

"One fing still puzzles me," said Spiffy.

"What's that?" I asked.

"Why does Wolfie tie a ribbon round 'is little log?"

"That, Spiffy," I said, "is quite a different case."

Black Sheep

Farmer Green had a lot of sheep, which spent all day in the field eating grass and saying "baaa". Not much of a life, but they seemed happy enough. I sometimes helped Bo-Peep to look after them. I enjoyed giving them orders and seeing them obey me. "Go over there," I'd say. "Over wheeeeere?" the sheep would ask. "Over by the tree," I'd say. "Yeeeees, Gideon," they'd bleat, and off they'd go to the tree. Great fun. If I told a sheep to stand on its head in a cowpat, I reckon it would. Sheep are the silliest animals I know.

But one day I met a sheep that was unlike any sheep I'd ever seen before. It came out from the trees, and it was black all over. I couldn't tell how much of the black was colour and how much was dirt, but if ever there was a black sheep, this was it. And quite apart from its blackness, it looked strange in other ways. Its coat was so long that it trailed along the ground, and its body seemed quite weighed down by the load. It also had something in its mouth.

"You're a funny-looking sheep," I said.

"Baaa," said the sheep, thereupon dropping what it was carrying, which turned out to be three bags.

"What are the bags for?" I asked.

"Woooool," said the sheep. "I have to taaaaake threeeee baaaaags fuuuuull."

"Three bags of wool?" I asked.

"One for the maaaaaster, one for the daaaaame, and one for the little boooooy that lives down the laaaaane," said the sheep.

83

He seemed to know what he was doing, and so I ordered him to get on with it. Bo-Peep was asleep under a haycock, but there was no need to wake her. This was something I could handle.

"Carry on," I said.

"Thaaaaank you, sir," he said.

I liked the way he called me "sir". He had the right attitude. I left him to collect his wool, and a short time later I saw him setting off towards the trees, dragging three bags along the ground. I wandered across.

"Got your wool, then?" I asked.

"Yes sir, yes sir," he said. 'Threeeee baaaaags fuuuuull."

One of the bags suddenly said "Meeeeeh!", but he quickly gave it a pull, and it went quiet again.

"No trouble, I hope," I said.

"No, sir," he said. "They gaaaaave me the woooool like laaaaambs."

I watched him disappear into the trees, and thought no more about it.

That evening, when it was time to go home, Bo-Peep counted the sheep as usual. Then she counted them again.

"Oh dear!" she said.

"What's the matter?" I asked.

"There are three lambs missing," she said. "Maybe they've wandered into the trees."

But they hadn't wandered into the trees. They hadn't wandered anywhere. One of the ewes said she'd seen the black sheep put three lambs into bags and drag them away.

"What black sheep?" asked Bo-Peep.

I told her all about the strange visitor.

"But you needn't worry," I told her. "He'd only come to collect some wool: one bag for the master, one for the dame, and one for the little boy who lives down the lane."

"What little boy?" asked Bo-Peep.

It wasn't an easy question to answer. The only person who lived down the lane was Old Mother Hubbard, but she didn't have any little boys with her. All she had was her dog.

Bo-Peep started to cry. Farmer Green would be very angry if we went home without the three lambs. Bo-Peep even blamed me for not waking her up, although I explained to her that the black sheep had obviously known what he was doing, and I'd had no problem handling the matter on my own. In fact I'd been doing her a favour by *not* waking her up.

"If you want to do me a favour," she said, "you'll find the three lambs."

It was another case for Gander of the Yard.

I quickly worked it out that my best chance of finding the lambs was to find the black sheep. But where was he? In all detective work, you need to take statements from witnesses, and so I set about questioning some of the sheep. They all said the same thing: "He went into the treeeees, draaaaagging the baaaaags behind him."

This was true. I'd seen it for myself. Therefore the sheep were not lying. On the other hand, if he'd dragged the bags into the trees, why weren't they there now?

"Why don't you fly up over the trees," suggested Bo-Peep, "and search from there?"

It didn't seem a very clever idea to me.

"They won't be up there," I said. "Sheep can't fly."

"But you can look down," said Bo-Peep, "and see a lot more of the ground from up there."

Now this *was* an idea. If I flew over the trees, I might be able to see something I couldn't see from the ground.

"Right!" I said. "Wait here, Bo-Peep. I'll soon find your lambs for you."

I took off and had just reached the first tree when I heard a familiar voice.

" 'Allo, Giddy."

It was Spiffy. He was sitting on a branch.

"On a case, are yer?" he asked.

I quickly told him about the black sheep and the missing lambs.

"Oh, them," he said. "Yes, sorry about that."

"Sorry about what?" I asked.

"Well, it was me, wasn't it?" he said.

"What was you?" I asked.

"It was me wot took 'em away," he said. "I'm a lambnapper."

This was unexpected. I looked closely at Spiffy. "You certainly don't look like a black sheep," I said.

"Course I don't!" he said. "An' I might be strong,

but I ain't strong enuff ter carry free lambs. No, mate, it was me wot was drivin' the black sheep. Didn't yer see me sittin' be'ind 'is ear'ole?"

I hadn't.

"I was tellin' 'im wot ter do. Yer know wot these sheep are like. Give 'em an order, an' they'll do it like you was the King 'isself."

It was true. I'd noticed that as well. It looked as if I was in luck.

"All right, Spiffy," I said. "Tell me where the lambs are."

"I can't," he said.

"Why not?" I asked.

"Cos I don't know," he said.

Maybe I wasn't so lucky after all. But Gideon Gander doesn't give up so easily.

"In that case," I said, "do you know where the black sheep is?"

"Yes," he said.

My luck was changing.

"Where?" I asked.

"Down there," he said, pointing with his left wing.

I looked down, and to my amazement saw the dirty black woollen coat far below, close to a blackberry bush.

"Well done, Spiffy!" I cried. "Find the sheep, find the lambs!"

I flew down at once to interrogate the black sheep. But the black sheep wasn't there. His coat was there, but there was no sheep inside it. Just a dirty black coat.

Spiffy had flown down with me.

"Can you explain this, Spiffy?" I asked.

"Ah!" said Spiffy. "Well, let's see . . . 'E did say 'e was feelin' a bit 'ot. That's right. 'E said 'e was 'ot, so 'e took 'is coat off an' left it 'ere."

"Then where did he go?" I asked.

"Dunno," said Spiffy. "But 'e shouldn't be 'ard ter find. There ain't many naked black sheep runnin' around the country."

He was right, and he was wrong. There might not have been many naked black sheep, but this one was very hard to find. He couldn't have been harder to find if he'd been invisible. I flew back to have another word with Spiffy. After all, if he'd been driving the sheep, he ought to know where the sheep had gone.

"No, mate," he said, "I don't."

"What were the last words you said to him, Spiffy?" I asked.

"I told 'im ter get lost," said Spiffy.

And that, of course, explained why I couldn't find him.

This was worrying. If I couldn't find the lambs, Bo-Peep would get into trouble with Farmer Green. What was even more worrying was that *I* could get into trouble with Farmer Green. But then an interesting thought occurred to me: if Spiffy stole the lambs, then Spiffy could get into trouble with Farmer Green. I mentioned this thought to Spiffy, and noticed a sudden change in his attitude.

"Oh!" he said.

"In fact, Spiffy," I went on, "Farmer Green would probably shoot you."

"In that case," said Spiffy, "I 'ave got somefink ter tell yer."

My heart rose.

"I never 'ad nuffink ter do wiv it."

My heart fell.

"I was makin' it all up," said Spiffy. "I mean, wot would I be doin' wiv free lambs? It's as much as I c'n do ter swaller a few breadcrumbs."

This was not the first time I had proved Spiffy to be a fibber, but on this occasion I wasn't very pleased. It left only Bo-Peep and me sharing the blame.

"I spend more time proving you innocent, Spiffy," I complained, "than proving the criminal guilty."

"Sorry, Giddy," he said. "I'm just a pafferlogical liar."

"I don't know about pafferlogical," I said — which was the truth, because I'd never heard of it — "but you certainly are a liar."

Proving Spiffy to be a liar, however, was no way to get the lambs back, and so I did the only thing left for me to do. I went to see Wolfie. Of course Wolfie didn't look like a black sheep, but I thought he might be interested in three missing lambs.

"Three missing lambs?" echoed Wolfie. "Three missing breakfasts, lunches and suppers? Let me find them, Goosey, and they'll be even more missing than they are now."

"Where are they, Wolfie?" I asked.

"If only I knew!" said Wolfie.

"What about the black sheep?" I asked.

"I'll have him for a black snack," he said. "Where is he?"

"That's what I'm asking you," I said.

At that moment I heard a strange sound coming from behind a bush. It was a sort of "meeeeeh meeeeeh".

"What's that noise?" I asked.

"What's what noise?" asked Wolfie.

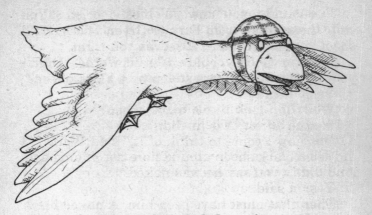

"Meeeeeh meeeeeh," said the noise.

"That sounds like lambs," I said.

"Never!" scoffed Wolfie. "Lambs say 'beeeeeh beeeeeh'."

"Beeeeeh beeeeeh," said the noise.

"Those are lambs!" I cried.

"I have to admit," said Wolfie, "they do sound like lambs."

I flew high over his head to the other side of the bush, and there I found three wriggling bags, all saying "meeeeeh" or possibly "beeeeeh".

91

"I've caught you now, Wolfie!" I cried. "You stole these lambs from Farmer Green's flock. He'll shoot you for this, and it serves you right."

"Hold on, Goosey, hold on," said Wolfie. "Didn't you say the lambs were stolen by a black sheep?"

"Yes," I said.

"Well, do I look like a black sheep?"

I had to admit that he didn't.

"But now I come to think of it," said Wolfie, "I did see a black sheep around here not so long ago. And didn't you say he was naked?"

"Yes," I said.

"Then that must have been him. A naked black sheep. He was carrying three bags. Are the lambs in bags, Goosey?"

"Yes," I said.

"Then it must have been the same black sheep. He asked me if I could tell him the way to the lane."

"The lane?" I asked.

"Yeah. He had to deliver three bags of wool — one to the master, one to the dame, and one to the little boy who lived down the lane."

I gasped. It was the same story the black sheep had told me. For once it seemed that Wolfie was telling the truth.

"What happened next, Wolfie?" I asked.

"I told him the way," said Wolfie. "What else would I do? And now you're telling me that dirty old sheep had stolen Farmer Green's lambs. Why, that's terrible. I should have stopped him. But wait. Let's think. Maybe I did stop him! Or maybe, Goosey, he heard *you* coming. Of course! He heard you coming, got scared, dropped the lambs behind the bush, and ran away. And I never noticed. Isn't that a stroke of luck?"

It *was* a stroke of luck. Now I could take the lambs back, and Bo-Peep and I wouldn't get into trouble.

"It's lucky for you, Wolfie," I said. "If I hadn't come along and scared the black sheep away, and then solved this whole mystery, you could have been shot."

"Yeah yeah," said Wolfie, "you're a great detective."

I was glad he appreciated it.

I untied the bags, and the lambs all jumped out and said "meeeeeh meeeeeh" and "thaaaaank you for saaaaaving us from Wolfie."

"Hey hey," said Wolfie, "I'm the good guy here. I saved you from the nasty black sheep."

A strange aspect of this case was that all the way home the lambs kept thanking me for saving them from Wolfie. I explained to them over and over again that it was the black sheep that had taken them away. I even took them to see the dirty coat which the black sheep had taken off when it had got too hot. But they just went on saying that Wolfie had been wearing it, and Wolfie had taken it off, and Wolfie would have eaten them.

"You lambs do talk nonsense," I said. "Whoever heard of a wolf in sheep's clothing?"

They still wouldn't believe me, but as I said at the beginning of this story, sheep are the silliest animals I know.

Fiddlers Three

As the greatest of all detectives, I am sometimes called on to solve cases in other parts of the world. And whenever the King has a problem, he naturally calls on me. I wish he wouldn't, but he does.

One day, soon after the case of Georgie Porgie, the King sent a message that I should go to the palace. I hate going there because he always makes me dig his garden. I sent a message back to the King that I had a terrible headache. Back came a message that the King had a special way of removing headaches.

"What's that?" I asked the messenger.

"Removing heads," he said.

And so I went to the palace.

"Ah, Goose," said the King, "I've got some work for you."

My digging muscles were beginning to ache already, but it turned out that this time the King had a case for me to solve.

"It's not for me," he said. "It's for the Queen's father – Old King Cole, over in Gotham. The Queen should be telling you this, but she's busy in the parlour eating bread and pâté de foie gras. Know what that is?"

I didn't, but superdetectives are supposed to know everything.

"Yeno," I said.

"Goose liver paste," said the King. "Her absolute favourite. Trouble is, you can't get the fresh goose liver these days. You haven't got any to spare, have you? Anyway, if you don't solve this case, I'll let the Queen have your liver, right? She'd probably prefer your liver to a solution, but still . . . Off you go. What are you waiting for?"

I was waiting because I couldn't move. Something out of my liver must have paralysed my legs and wings.

"I suppose you want to know how to get to Gotham," he said.

"Yes, please, Your Majesty," I said.

"You fly. That's what your wings are for."

"Yes, Your Majesty."

"You want to know where it is?"

"Yes, please, Your Majesty."

"Turn left at Totham, right at Spotham, up to Shotham, down to Potham and Gotham's at the bottom of Rotham. Good luck, Goose, and report back with your liver if you fail to solve the case."

It took me four hours to find Gotham. It wasn't at the bottom of Rotham. It was at the top of Potham.

I went straight to the palace, where I found an old gentleman lying on the floor in his underwear, smoking a pipe and resting his bare feet in a bowl of water.

"Hello, old gentleman," I said. "I'm looking for King Cole."

'Ho ho ho," he said. He was a merry old soul. "And who might you be?"

"I'm Gideon Gander, the famous detective," I replied.

"Ho ho ho," he said. "Well, I'm King Cole."

This was a surprise. Kings usually wear crowns and a badge that says KING – at least, our King does.

"Ho ho ho, sit down," he said.

I looked for a chair, but there weren't any. In fact, there was no furniture of any kind. The whole place was completely bare.

"Ah!" said the King. "Nowhere to sit, eh? Ho ho ho. Well, that's my problem. Someone's been stealing my furniture. And not just my furniture. I've lost my crown, my badge, my throne, my tables, chairs, pictures – everything. Nothing left now except the underclothes I lie down in, and my pipe and my bowl. Ho ho ho."

It didn't seem all that funny to me. He was going to ask me to find the thief, and if I didn't, our King would give my liver to the Queen.

"I want you to find the thief," he said, "and when you find him, I'll make you a baronet. How's that? Ho ho ho."

Now that did interest me. I've always wanted a title, and being a baronet would really suit me. Everyone would have to call me sir, then, including Wolfie.

"Right, Your Majesty," I said, "I'll take the case."

"Haven't got any cases," he said. "They stole them, too, ho ho ho."

It was a bit difficult to tell with all this ho-ho-hoing whether the King was really making a joke or being serious. So I laughed and frowned at the same time, and said, "Hoahemm, hoahemm."

What I now needed to know was who had stolen all the King's things.

"Your Majesty," I asked, "have you any idea who has stolen your things?"

"No," he said. "Have you? Ho ho ho."

"No," I said. "Hoahemm, hoahemm. Now, Your Majesty, have you by any chance seen a wolf anywhere around the palace?"

"No," he said. "Should I have done? Ho ho ho."

"Hoahemm, hoahemm," I said.

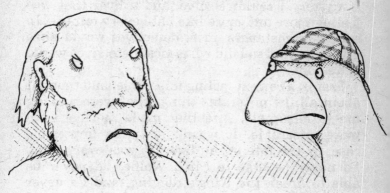

"Why do you keep going hoahemm, hoahemm?" he asked. "Something wrong with your throat, ho ho ho?"

"No, not at all," I said.

"Then stop doing it," he said. "It's a silly noise, ho ho ho." Perhaps he wasn't such a merry old soul after all. Perhaps he was really a dangerous old soul. You can never tell with Kings.

"Certainly, Your Majesty," I said. "Now I'd better get on and interview the suspects."

Unfortunately, if there wasn't a wolf around, I didn't have any suspects.

"What about the servants?" I asked.

"What about what servants?" he asked. "All gone, ho ho ho. My money was stolen, so I couldn't pay 'em and they left."

I wandered off to look round the palace for clues. There were no clues. There was nothing and nobody in the palace. It was as empty as Gary the Gosling's head. There I was, worn out after my long flight, hungry, thirsty, alone in this bare palace in this strange town with a ho-hoing king, a mystery I couldn't solve, and a liver that was feeling more and more like pâté every minute. In such circumstances, most detectives would have given up. And so I did what most detectives would have done.

I sat in a corner, feeling miserable, and thought about all the miserable things that were making me so miserable. And that made me feel even more miserable. It wasn't just this impossible case, or the fate of my liver. It was everything. I'd never be able to catch Wolfie, I'd never be able to finish the King's digging, and I'd never be able to teach Gary anything. Only if I could get rid of these misery-making miseries would I escape from misery, but how do you get rid of master criminals and head-chopping kings and idiot goslings?

"Say that again," I said to myself.

How do you get rid of master criminals and head-chopping kings and idiot goslings?

There was an idea trying to form itself in my mind. Somehow it was connected with King Cole's missing belongings.

"Think!" said my mind. "Think!"

"I'm trying," I said.

But the more I thought, the less connected the connection became. Back I went into my misery, but for some reason I had stood up, and now I wandered aimlessly out of the palace and off along the road. Perhaps I was hoping to find food, or drink, or a clue, or a quiet death.

At the side of the road was a man with a barrow. It was a big barrow, and on it were pictures, ornaments, clothes and pieces of furniture.

"Come an' buy!" he was shouting. "Ev'ryfink must go! Bargain prices, an' all good quality stuff, straight from the King's own palace!"

I went across to have a closer look. I spotted a picture of King Cole himself, smoking his pipe, and I noticed that every item had a label saying "Property of His Majesty King Cole".

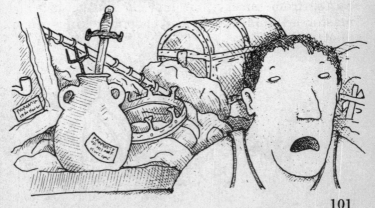

"Wanner buy somefink, Goosey?" the man asked.

He was tall, dark, with a long nose and shifty eyes. Something about him reminded me of Wolfie.

"Ev'ryfink goin' cheap," he said.

Something else about him reminded me of Spiffy.

"I gotter get rid of it all," he said.

And suddenly my mind made the connection it had been trying to form earlier. Whoever stole the King's belongings would have to get rid of them! He might even try to sell them.

"'Ow 'bout this luvley gold crown, then?" said the Wolfie–Spiffy man. "Wear it roun' yer neck, an' people'll fink yer a dog."

Could this man have something to do with the crime? I knew I would have to phrase my questions very carefully.

"Tell me, my man," I said, "where did you steal these things from?"

His reply was not quite what I had expected.

"Steal 'em, guv'nor?" he cried. "I never stole nuffink!"

It was a disappointment. If he had confessed, I could have taken him to the King, collected my baronetiness, saved my liver, and gone home.

"Are you sure?" I asked.

"I never stole nuffink in me life!" repeated the man. "As sure as my name's 'Onest Joe."

This was puzzling. Someone had stolen the King's belongings, Honest Joe was selling them, and yet he hadn't stolen them. It was another of those connections that wouldn't quite connect.

"Very well," I said, "if you didn't steal them, who did?"

"Nobody," he said.

It was another unexpected reply. The King had said they were stolen, but Honest Joe said they were not. Could the King be lying? Or was it possible that these were not the King's belongings after all?

What I did next was masterly. I bought the gold crown. It cost me six precious and painful feathers, but since I was going to be a baronet, a gold crown would come in very handy. Besides, I would now be able to find out whether Honest Joe was really selling the King's belongings or not.

"Suits yer, Goosey," said Honest Joe. "Woof woof!"

I returned to the palace, where Old King Cole was still lying on the ground with his pipe in his mouth and his feet in the bowl.

"Found the thief yet, ho ho ho?" he asked.

"No, Your Majesty," I said.

"Then what's my gold crown doing round your neck, ho ho ho?"

He had made a bad mistake.

"It's not your gold crown, Your Majesty," I said.

"It's mine."

"Nonsense," he said. "Look at the label: 'Property of His Majesty King Cole', ho ho ho."

"It *was* yours, Your Majesty," I said, "but I've just bought it, and so now it's mine."

"If you don't take it off this minute," said King Cole, "you'll find yourself without a neck to hang it on, ho ho ho."

Kings are the same everywhere. I took the crown off and gave it to him. It was like giving him six precious, painful feathers.

"Now," he said, "where did you get it?"

I told him about the man with the barrow.

"Then he's the thief, ho ho ho!" shouted the King. "Go and arrest him!"

"No, he's not the thief," I said. "He's Honest Joe, and he's never stolen anything in his life."

"If he's not the thief," said the King, "he must have got it from the thief, so find out who he got it from, ho ho ho."

Clues often come from the most unexpected sources. This chance remark of the King's enabled me to form a completely new theory. If Honest Joe had not stolen the crown, perhaps he had got it from someone who had. I only had to find out who Honest Joe had got the crown from, and then I would know the identity of the thief. This was detection at its finest.

I rushed out of the palace to look for Honest Joe, but he had disappeared. He'd probably finished work for the day. But not for nothing do we ganders have wings. I took off, circled over Gotham, and spotted Honest Joe heading in the direction of a large house on a hill. He was quite surprised to see me.

"There was nuffink wrong wi' that crown," he said. "That was best quality, that was. An' if you lost it, it ain't my fault."

"I haven't lost it, Honest Joe," I said. "I gave it back to the King."

His eyes went wide, his mouth fell open, and his face turned pale.

"You give it back ter the King?" he cried.

"And now," I said, "I want you to tell me who you got it from."

"Well," he said, "um . . . well . . . I got it from where I gets all the uvver stuff."

"Where do you get the uvver stuff?" I asked.

"Um . . . from them," he said.

"Who's them?" I asked.

He looked left, then right, then behind him, then above him, then behind me, then round me, then up the road, down the road, and round the corner. I had a feeling that he didn't want anyone else to hear.

"The free wise men," he whispered.

"Free wise men?" I repeated.

"Shh!" he hissed.

"Where will I find them?" I asked.

"In that 'ouse. Only don't tell 'em I told yer."

The house was the one on the hill. I said good-bye to Honest Joe, who hurried away in the opposite direction, and then I flew to the front door. It had a nameplate on it, saying "Twee, Tweedle and Tweedle Dee, financial advisers by appointment to His Majesty the King". I rang the doorbell.

The door was opened by a tall man in black suit and tie, wearing a badge that said "Jenkins, butler by appointment to His Majesty the King". He looked out over my head.

"Good afternoon," I said.

He looked down.

"Good heavens," he said.

"Very well," I said, "good heavens, if you prefer it. Are you Mr Twee, Mr Tweedle, or Mr Tweedle Dee?"

"I am Jenkins the Butler," he replied.

"Correct," I said. (He did not know that I had read his badge.) "My name is Gideon Gander."

He should have said, "Oh, the famous detective." But he didn't.

"I'm the famous detective," I said. At least one of us had said it. "And I'm here on behalf of His Majesty the King."

"Who is it?" "Who is it?" "Who is it?" asked three different voices from three different directions.

The butler told them three times who it was, and then from out of three different rooms came three little men, all looking exactly the same. They were short and fat, bald and bespectacled, and were wearing pin-striped trousers and waistcoats.

"From His Majesty the King?" "From His Majesty the King?" "From His Majesty the King?" they asked.

"Yes. Yes. Yes," I replied.

"He'd better come in." "He'd better come in." "He'd better come in."

The butler told me to come in, and asked the three little men which room I should go to. There were three lots of discussions, and then I was taken into a long gallery which was full of paintings and furniture labelled "Property of His Majesty King Cole". We all sat round one of the tables.

"How is His Majesty?" "How is His Majesty?" "How is His Majesty?" they asked.

I told them three times that His Majesty wasn't very happy, and each of them in turn said "Tut tut" and giggled.

Then they asked me three times why I'd come, and I explained that I was investigating the theft of His Majesty's property. I thought that, as they were the King's financial advisers, they might be able to help me.

"What a pity!" "What a pity!" "What a pity!" they said.

It turned out, as they told me three times, that they were no longer the King's financial advisers, and they really must take that nameplate down from the door. At this they all giggled again.

"So we can't help you." "We can't help you." "We can't help you," they said.

It was clear that if they no longer worked at the palace, they were unlikely to know who had stolen the King's property. On the other hand, why did they have the King's property in their house? Once again, there was a connection here that I couldn't quite connect.

"It's been lovely meeting you." "It's been lovely meeting you." "It's been lovely meeting you," they said, and I was just getting ready to leave them when there came a very dramatic interruption. The butler opened the door, and announced, "His Majesty the King."

Then in doddered Old King Cole himself. The three little men went as white as my feathers, leapt to their feet, and bent themselves double.

"Aha!" shouted the King. "Oho oho oho!"

Behind him were three large policemen.

"There they are!" shouted the King. "All my belongings, ho ho ho! Arrest these men, officers, and take them away!"

"But — " "But — " "But — " cried the three wise men, as the three policemen took one each and carried them out of the room.

"Well done, Goose," said the King. "You've done a fine job, ho ho ho."

This was a surprise to me, but the whole case had been full of surprises, so another surprise was scarcely surprising.

The King and I then made a tour of the whole house, and in all the rooms we found furniture and valuables labelled "Property of His Majesty King Cole", while down in the servants' quarters we even found dozens of people wearing badges that said "Servants to His Majesty King Cole". The King ordered all of them to go back to the palace, and to take his property with them.

Out in the stables, the King found his coach, his coachman and his horses, and he invited me to drive back to the palace with him. I would spend the night there, and in the morning he would make me a baronet. This I found very exciting, though I was still a little puzzled about what was going on. It wasn't, for instance, quite clear to me who exactly had been the thief.

On the way back to the palace, the King told me what had happened. Honest Joe had gone to the palace and told His Majesty that the three wise men had given him all the King's property to sell. He, Honest Joe, had had no idea that the property was stolen. When the great detective (that was me) had got on the trail, he had sent him (me again) to the big house on the hill.

"So I fetched the police," said the King, "and followed you there. Caught them all red-handed, ho ho ho."

And then the King told me something that at last enabled me to solve the whole mystery.

"Those three men had been fiddling the accounts for years. They were in charge of all my money, you see, and bit by bit they took everything away till I had nothing left. And then they all retired to the house on the hill, ho ho ho."

It didn't take me long to work out the final detail of this case. There had not been one thief at all. There had been three: the three wise men of Gotham. Wise they may have been, but they had been no match for Gander of the Yard.

That night I slept in a four-poster bed, but I kept having nightmares about myself running around in nothing but pimples. It turned out that my duvet was filled with goose feathers.

The following morning, the King sent for me. He was sitting on his throne, wearing his crown and his badge.

"Morning, Goose," he said. "It's a great day. Time to get started, ho ho ho."

He called for his pipe, lit it, and called for his bowl. I wondered what he was going to do with it. Then he called for the three wise men.

"So," he said, "my financial advisers, eh? Ho ho ho. Fiddlers three. And each of you fiddlers had a fiddle, and a very fine fiddle you had, eh, Twee, Tweedle, and Tweedle Dee. Well, you've fiddled your last fiddle, all of you. See this bowl? Well, my three wise men of Gotham, you will go to sea in this bowl. And since it's not very strong, your voyage won't be long, ho ho ho."

When the three wise men and the bowl had been taken away, the King turned to me – the hero of the story. It was a wonderful moment.

"Now then, Goose," he said, "it's time for your reward. I'm going to make you a baronet."

He clapped his hands, and in came Honest Joe. He was carrying a big ball of string, which he held out in front of the King. The King took some of the strands in his hands, and began to weave them together. It must have been part of the official ceremony, but it seemed to go on for a very long time. At last, though, the King was ready.

"Here you are, Goose," he said, and I approached the throne. "Hold out your wings."

I held out my wings, and he placed the string over them.

"Congratulations," he said. "You've earned this. Goodbye, and good luck, ho ho ho."

I thanked him, though I didn't quite know what for.

"Not at all, not at all," he said. "Off you go, ho ho ho."

I left the palace, and Honest Joe left with me.

"Yer don't really want that, do yer?" he asked.

"I don't know," I said. "What is it?"

"'Ere," he said. "I'll show yer."

He took it from me, and we walked up the road. There he spread the string all over his barrow.

"See?" he said. "It's a barrer net. Very useful fer us as 'as a barrer."

The King hadn't made me a baronet. He'd made me a barrow net. I gave it to Honest Joe, and in return he gave me a pile of labels that said "Property of His Majesty King Cole". I didn't think they would be much use to me, but he seemed particularly keen that I should take them away with me. I still don't really know why.

The End

David Henry Wilson
Gander of the Yard £2.99

Was Humpty Dumpty pushed?
Who really killed Cock Robin?
What happened to the sheep while
Little Bo Peep was asleep?

The world's greatest mysteries cry out for the world's greatest
detective. And Gideon Gander, husband of Mother Goose, is the
sleuth for the truth!

There's a Wolf in my Pudding £2.99

Was Red Riding Hood really such an angel?
Who was disguised as a prince disguised as a frog?
Why did a gangster help the tortoise beat the hare?

Get ready for laughter, lies, suspense and surprise as you learn
the terrible truth behind a dozen famous tales.

Yucky Ducky £2.99

Do not read this book. It contains tales of the yuckiest duck that
ever quacked, the wickedest wolf that ever howled and the
stupidest ostrich that never flew.
You'll hate the hyena that wouldn't laugh, you'll loathe the
leopard that wouldn't eat meat, and you'll elefume at the
elephant that eleforgot. These animals are crazy. So do not read
this book.
Unless you feel like having a good laugh.

All Pan books are available at your local bookshop or newsagent, or can be ordered direct from the publisher. Indicate the number of copies required and fill in the form below.

Send to: Pan C. S. Dept
              Macmillan Distribution Ltd
              Houndmills Basingstoke RG21 2XS
or phone: 0256 29242, quoting title, author and Credit Card number.

Please enclose a remittance* to the value of the cover price plus: £1.00 for the first book plus 50p per copy for each additional book ordered.

*Payment may be made in sterling by UK personal cheque, postal order, sterling draft or international money order, made payable to Pan Books Ltd.

Alternatively by Barclaycard/Access/Amex/Diners

Card No. ⬚⬚⬚⬚⬚⬚⬚⬚⬚⬚⬚⬚⬚⬚⬚⬚⬚⬚⬚

Expiry Date ⬚⬚⬚⬚⬚⬚

_____

                        Signature:

Applicable only in the UK and BFPO addresses

While every effort is made to keep prices low, it is sometimes necessary to increase prices at short notice. Pan Books reserve the right to show on covers and charge new retail prices which may differ from those advertised in the text or elsewhere.

NAME AND ADDRESS IN BLOCK LETTERS PLEASE:

....

Name_____

Address_____

_____

_____

_____

                                                              6/92